A
RAMBLER
STEALS
HOME

A RAMBLER STEALS HOME

CARTER HIGGINS

HOUGHTON MIFFLIN HARCOURT
Boston New York

www.hmhco.com

The text was set in Chaparral Pro Light.
Title page art © 2017 by Brandon Dorman
Book design by Sharismar Rodriguez

Library of Congress Cataloging-in-Publication Data is available.
ISBN 978-0-544-60201-4

Manufactured in the United States of America
DOC 10 9 8 7 6 5 4 3 2 1
4500639412

For my dad, who took me to all those minor-league baseball games

A
RAMBLER
STEALS
HOME

JUNE 6

One

AREN'T we lucky?" Garland asked. "Just traveling souls, making traditions and cheeseburgers."

"Lucky," I said right back. I didn't really know if I believed that part, but I sure could believe in the summer's traditions.

Garland always said being a rambler of the road meant three things: food, family, and fun. Triple and I always said it meant three other things: blisters, grease splatters, and loneliness. But there we were, rambling back into Ridge Creek for another summer.

The Rambler's windows were down, and a hot breeze gave away the hiding place of a skunk out in a roadside ditch. Garland sang at the top of his lungs, sounding like someone who should stick to doing it in the shower. And since he was driving the Rambler, he was almost in reaching distance of our shower stall, so I guess that counted. Triple played along on his banjo, which wasn't really a banjo—it was just an empty shoebox with a paper towel tube for a neck and rubber bands for strings. Garland had gotten real mad when he found out Triple used the good scissors to cut a hole in the lid, but that shoebox was worth saving. Triple had named him Twang. I didn't want to admit to either one of them how much I liked their broken duet.

So as we bumped along the country roads, the three of us stretched our necks around to rest our eyes on the landmarks. It was a routine that told us the rambling was about to settle down. It would slow to a complete stop for the summer, and so would we.

While Garland and I counted landmarks, Triple sang, making up new words for the stories we knew by heart. There was the old drive-in: *"Roll down the windows of your car, set your eyes on a movie star!"* The farm with all those calm cows that stood staring together, always in the same direction: *"Bales to the east; moos to the west!"* And of course, the general store that sold gigantic concrete planters that looked just like turkeys: *"Mister Mayflower sticks his zinnias in his fancy turkey dinn-ias!"*

Once Garland kicked in the parking brake and unhooked the Grill from the back of the Rambler, we wouldn't see the drive-in or the cows or the turkeys. We'd stay close to the Grill all summer, because even though we were done with the driving for a while, we weren't done with the work. But that would be okay, because we'd be right in the shadow of the best baseball stadium there ever was. We'd have traditions and time and each other. Besides, I always did prefer summer grease splatters to winter blisters, and the next few months would be full of those hot, prickly burns.

If only I could've counted on grease splatters to be the biggest trouble of the season.

Two

OF all the times we piled up in the Rambler, summer was my favorite. The bleachers weren't all that great for your hind parts, but at least they were bolted in one place.

Triple liked the springtime's rambling, but I think that was mostly because you couldn't drive anywhere without hitting some kind of carnival, and he would've been happy eating cotton candy for every meal of the day. That's how it is when you're seven, and Garland didn't seem to mind like maybe a mama would.

Garland, our papa, liked the turning of the leaves up north when it was the cider and sweater time of year. Then, right after the pumpkins got all smashed up and you'd have pies coming out your ears, it was time for Christmas trees. That tightrope of a drive along Canada's edge and west to Wisconsin got a little tricky because our Rambler wasn't exactly made for snow tires, but that was Garland's favorite of the rambling seasons. That's when he laughed the most.

Hauling Christmas trees out of a Wisconsin forest made for some juicy blisters, no thanks to scraggly mittens that let icicles and pine needles poke through. The woods were right off a four-lane highway where all that broke the black of night were white lights coming and red lights going. We just lived right there in our Rambler, parked in the roadside lot, where most people only stayed long enough to pick out a tree. It was a whole lot of hard work to give someone else something to hang tinsel and candy canes on.

Every winter, Garland said, "Aren't we lucky? We get more Christmas trees than anyone could fit in their home, even if they were the president or the queen."

I'd still love to have just one.

And that one tree would be in one home.

Ours.

Garland's love of the season is why my middle name is Christmas. He said didn't he get lucky, having a name like Garland and then finding the Christmas-tree business? He took it as a sign, but I thought it was probably just a coincidence.

I'd never tell him that.

Even though we rambled, we always had one moneymaker hitched up to the back of our Rambler —and that's where the grease came from. That old concession stand trailer had been Garland's Grill since he bought it at a flea market in the middle of Oklahoma. The man with the cash box said it was only fit to stay in place and maybe serve up cold-cut sandwiches and cans of soda, but Garland had a bigger vision. He saw wheels that worked, and a fryer that was new to us even though it came from an old fast-food restaurant somewhere in Indiana—and, of course, he saw Christmastime. Even when the summer sweated, he tied up strands of fake greenery and Christmas lights on the front of Garland's Grill, then knotted it all up with a floppy red bow. I don't know if he was jolly because he loved Christmas so much or if it was the other way around.

Everywhere we went, Garland changed what we served at the Grill. The Christmas-tree people lined up for hot chocolate and gingersnaps, and on sweater days it was apple cider and cinnamon-sugar-too-sweet donuts. All up and down those spring highways, it was snacks and bottles of water.

And no matter where we were, when we were done for the day, Garland still made us do school right there in the Rambler. "Aren't we lucky," he said, "making up the things we want to learn and doing it as we go?" He was a lot of things to me and Triple: Our papa. Our boss. And our teacher. So I used to call him Mr. Clark to tease him. But one day I called him Garland to get his attention, and it just plain stuck.

I think he liked it, since it was what our mama used to call him.

After Triple had gotten his fill of carnival cotton candy every spring, it was time to get back to Virginia. We rode into town just in time to watch the Ridge Creek Rockskippers play ball from June to September. Garland's Grill set up shop right there in the parking lot of the James Edward Allen Gibbs Stadium, where its wheels didn't have to matter for a while. We'd fire up the fryer and get the burgers ready to flip and we didn't have to do school all summer.

"Poor little schnauzer stuck to the ground, won't ever chase his tail around!" sang Triple. The schnauzer

mailbox with the hanging ears and sweet eyes meant we were close. Garland and Triple rolled up the windows, since it was getting later and they were getting louder.

Every summer when we drove into town, we went the long way. Garland liked to ramble as long as we could before we got to that parking lot, like he didn't quite feel right with two feet on the ground. Maybe Garland was a little superstitious about sunsets, but for as long as I could remember, we got to Ridge Creek once it was already dark and everything was quiet.

The houses were mostly set way back from the main road, which must have made getting the mail a muddy run on rainy days, and you couldn't even connect a tin-can phone from your window to the one next door. Seemed like they were all wasting the best part of being neighbors.

There was the clearing to the creek, the one you had to wrestle tentacles of honeysuckle and Queen Anne's lace to get through. In the dark, it would be hard to know it was there, but we did anyway.

We passed the Sweet Street Mart, and I didn't

even have to be inside to smell the sour-pickle air about it.

The Heritage Inn was about the only thing around with its lights on, which was a good thing, since we'd circle back around to its parking lot to stay. It shared that parking lot and a bunch of stories with the stadium, and since it didn't have much in the way of room service, it was a real good place for us to end up. The people at the inn would get hungry, and we'd be right outside their front door shaking salt on fries.

But, like always, not before a slow drive past the James Edward Allen Gibbs Stadium. We may as well have parked, because each side of its entrance didn't stretch much farther than from the driver's seat of the Rambler to the tail end of Garland's Grill. Even though it was dark and I couldn't see the insides yet, I could feel what the place looked like. I could see the red paint of the giant ROCKSKIPPERS fading to the color of a mouse's tail, mostly on the ROCK part. A red-and-blue Rockskippers flag hung still and lonely in the thick, hot air, and right at the entrance was the box office, covered in pennants and hope and ghosts of the past. It was on wheels too, but it never left this place.

"Cool," Triple said. "I wonder if they finally got cotton candy."

"Maybe," I said, in a little bit of wonder myself.

"Hey, Derby, you promised you'd teach me that Rockskipper high-five, remember?" Triple said when we rolled past the tall banner, the one from the roof to the ground, the one that showed some of the first Rockskippers celebrating something great.

"Promise," I said.

Garland was looking up even higher. "Looks like Ferdie's working late tonight."

I leaned out to see. The man had a flashlight in his teeth, and he was aiming it way up above him at the stadium's marquee. He hadn't changed a bit in the last year, except for maybe being a little saggier in the shoulders. Some things are easy to spot, even in the almost-dark.

Ferdie's job as the stadium's caretaker made him the voice of that marquee, and otherwise he didn't say much. And like him, that big sign was quiet for the whole year, empty until the season started back up. Those letters meant life to the Rockskippers.

"What do you think it's gonna say?" Triple asked.

"Hard to tell," Garland said, but he studied every letter that was up there.

All I could make out was **SAVE**.

"The date, maybe?" I finished what Ferdie might have been starting. "But everyone knows that Opening Day is tomorrow."

"Maybe," Garland said, and picked up the Rambler's tempo.

"*Save* me the fastest turtle!" Triple added. He'd be sleepless over that on our first night back, getting to the creek in time for a good one first thing in the morning.

And just like that, the traditions were on.

Three

WE rattled onto the patch of concrete where the stadium parking lot ended and the Heritage Inn parking lot began. Garland let the engine idle for a minute before he turned it off.

"Here we are. Hit the hay." He'd aimed the front of the Rambler away from the stadium, so the driver's-seat window looked out toward the darkness.

Triple curled up on his bunk by the refrigerator, and Garland was being awful slow to stand up. I only had a few steps to walk between the passenger seat and my very own room, so that's where I went. Garland shared the double bunk with Triple, and they'd given me the whole queen bed in the back. It wasn't much, but Garland always said *Ladies first* and I did think that was really nice. It closed off to the rest of the Rambler with only a shower curtain and two crossed fingers, but at least I got my very own window. That gave me a straight-on view of the Heritage

Inn's front door, which was a handy place to keep a good eye on Betsy Plogger, who was never up to anything good.

"Night, Garland," I said.

He didn't reply.

I slid the shower curtain shut behind me, then pushed the little seahorse curtain away from the fogged-up window. My mama had made that curtain when I was real small, and she was better at a whole lot of things than sewing. The pattern didn't match up quite right, and the side facing out of the Rambler was faded, thanks to the highway sun. But that seahorse curtain was one true thing I could keep of her.

Out the window, in the fuzzy light of the Heritage Inn, I liked what I saw.

A big poster hung on the fence with something that looked like Christmas ribbons, and it spelled out its message with giant letters.

Welcome back, Sugar Sue

Sugar Sue.

Only one person called me that, and the sight of that permanent black marker pressed down by her own two hands made me itch. Or it might have been because we'd finally stopped moving, but there was a little extra tingle in whatever was traveling through my soul.

I squinted to read the rest. Underneath, it said

See you at the box office first thing.

Love, June.

My trusty old friend Marcus Emmett was one of the best parts of every summer. The other best part was June. June Mattingly.

June was the rock to the Rockskippers' skip. That box office, the one on wheels and covered in pennants, was her place. She sold tickets and was the first thing anyone saw before they marched into the stadium with their families and foam fingers. Most people thought she never left that little home on its stuck-down wheels, but I knew better.

We'd been friends since I was younger than Triple, since the summer Marcus dared me to sneak into the stadium. I got caught by Ferdie, who was the spit kind of mad, but June pretended like I was supposed to be there all along. That was the last summer my mama was a rambler, so after that, June was the one who knew when I moved from seahorses to sparkly things and when I changed my mind back again.

It was easy to see the glamour in a name like June Mattingly when yours was Derby Christmas Clark. It was hard enough being a rambler of the road without being named after some home-run contest.

So I'd been looking forward to our first morning in Ridge Creek mostly because of June. It was about time I got rid of those boys for a bit. Maybe she would finally show me how to put on lipstick. In the other years, we'd sit on her porch swing eating strawberries and drinking lemonade, and maybe if she could sneak them by Mr. Mattingly, she'd bring out his favorite oatmeal raisin cookies from somewhere inside.

"See you at the box office tomorrow," I said out loud.

Meeting June at the box office wasn't tradition at all, but if that's what she wanted, then that's what we'd do.

JUNE 7

Four

IT was barely light out when I woke up that first morning in the Rambler. My opening day in Ridge Creek was full of traditions: June in the morning, Marcus at the creek in the afternoon, the Rockskippers in the early evening, and Garland's Grill after. A whole summer of days like that was a welcome sight for a rambler.

But the problem with living in an RV in a parking lot was that there was no way to dump the toilets in any kind of civilized manner, so Betsy Plogger's Aunt Candy let us use the restrooms near the lobby in the Heritage Inn. Betsy lived at the inn year-round with the rest of the Ploggers, so she felt like she owned the place too. But it was Candy Plogger who ran the show, and if she said so, people listened. I thought she let us use those restrooms mostly because she was an old friend of my mama's and sometimes she felt a little bit sorry for us.

It was still early and I could probably avoid Betsy Plogger if I hurried, since I bet she was still getting some beauty sleep. So I snuck in the side door of the inn to use the ladies' room.

Glamorous.

By the time I got back to the Rambler, Triple and Garland were up and making eggs. "Protein for the pro team!" Garland would always say. Except this time he didn't, because he had a mouthful of breakfast.

"Turtle-catching today?" I asked Triple.

"I can smell the fast ones already," he said, kicking one anxious foot into the storage bench under our table, the one that seated four people.

"Eggs?" Garland wiped his hands on his shorts.

"No, thanks," I said. "I've got a date with June Mattingly." And I had my eye on strawberries and oatmeal raisin cookies instead.

"We'll prep before the game, okay?" Garland never let the Grill routine mess up my own, and I was awful grateful for that.

Triple dropped his plate in the sink and launched himself out of our flimsy front door. He took Twang with him, because although Twang made a great banjo, in a pinch he also did a really great job of housing turtles.

A smack-split second before I lost sight of his brown curls, he turned around and said, "Last one back does the onions!" We both hated doing the onions. Slicing them made you cry and frying them made a bunch of grease splatters. Still, like I said, I'd always preferred grease splatters to blisters.

The night before had been dark and still except for Ferdie and his flashlight, but in the steamy morning you could almost see some electricity in the air. Since the stadium was pretty much in our backyard, I didn't have to walk far to get to it, but I still wanted to go through it rather than around it.

I'd liked it that way ever since Marcus's dare.

So I waited in the space between right field's foul pole and some dusty gravel, right behind a sign that was stuck to the fence, as close to the wood as I could get. It didn't matter that the paint on the other side was peeling and faded, because I knew what it said even without seeing it: THE SWEET STREET MART, FILLING BELLIES AND HEARTS SINCE 1957. I slipped through the skinny hole between FILLING and BELLIES, where the boards were too bowed to stand up straight. Marcus had shown me that you had to suck in your gut to not get splinters, but once you breathed again, you'd be standing right there in right field.

Even though it was hours before the game, I could still feel this rickety old park's majesty. The charm of the Ridge Creek Rockskippers was never lost on me. Some of the kids in the Christmas-tree part of my life got a little snobby when it came to sports, what with the Milwaukee Brewers sharing their state and all. You could feed a family of eight at Garland's Grill for the cost of one plain old hot dog at a Brewers game, so I didn't really think that was something to brag about. I never did see what the big deal was about the big leagues.

This place was more like me. Maybe because it felt kinda nice that I was the one to stay put for a bit and the players were the ones on the road together.

Luckily, June Mattingly stayed put at the stadium all summer, even during away games. She had to, since her husband, Franklin, took good care of that grass, the green I was standing on in right field.

Franklin Mattingly had broad shoulders, massive hands, and an even bigger heart. Players came and went as they got good enough for the big leagues, and the teenagers that sold peanuts and pretzels night after night left for college. But Franklin Mattingly was always there. The first to show up and the last to leave.

He had been the groundskeeper since the year the James Edward Allen Gibbs Stadium was built, and it belonged more to him than anyone who ever wore a Rockskippers uniform. He was why center field and left field looked just as good as the one I was on. He was why even the dirt sparkled. He was also why June Mattingly smiled so big that some of her lipstick shimmied down and stained her front teeth.

Halfway through the fifth inning at every game, Franklin would drive June around on his cart as it smoothed the infield, and they would hop out at second base and dance. They didn't depend on the ballpark organ for the rhythm; they just made up whatever felt good, I guess. Some nights it was a calm kind of boogie and other nights it was a flailing type of jive, but my most favorite nights were the slow dances. June always kissed the top of Franklin's shoulder and they stood there, just for a moment. And after their dance, they'd hop back in the cart and continue as if nothing had ever happened.

Games like that made me forget about the onions and annoying Betsy Plogger and the table for four in our Rambler. Maybe we *were* lucky, getting to watch baseball and sunsets every summer.

But then the sprinklers *ch-ch-chhhhhh*ed on without any warning, spraying me with water from all angles. June wouldn't care if I looked a little unruly. I could be wearing a prom dress or a grease-splattered T-shirt and she would still call me Sugar Sue.

"Careful!" Ferdie's voice carried across the infield. "Grounds crew won't want to clean up your mud prints!"

I nodded over in his direction, toward third base, both because I didn't want to give Franklin more cleanup work and because I didn't really want to get much wetter either. And I didn't even mind that I'd gotten caught sneaking in again. It would be a good story to tell Marcus later.

So I raced down the first-base line. Dirt and chalk flew up and stuck to my wet legs, making a slimy mess all the way up to my knees. I didn't mind that, either.

I jumped on home plate for good luck, waited until I heard three clanks of Old Glory waving wildly into

her pole, and then ran my hands along the net behind home plate to find the strings where the knots
had come loose. And then I used Marcus's secret
hold-your-breath trick and executed a very ungrace-
ful belly-slide under the bleachers.

Five

THE inside walkways of the James Edward Allen Gibbs Stadium cast the same kind of spell as the outfield. They smelled like peanut butter from all the smashed and salted shells, which was almost as delicious a smell as the one in Franklin's field.

The day was still quiet, but getting louder. There were some pops and cracks of gloves as the Rockskippers began to take the field for drills, and a cluster of pigeons poked around for stray peanuts. They'd have more luck once the season was in full swing, because for now the stadium was looking almost brand-new again.

June's tiny hut always made our Rambler look like some real queen's quarters, but her place was just as special. Rockskippers pennants earned in seasons past covered it from the shingles to the ground —always blue and red, some more weathered than others. They were familiar and faded, like some kind of home.

I heard her singing something a little bit hushed inside her box office. And then, there she was. June came out with two lemonades and a grin. "Hey there, Sugar Sue. I've been waiting for you."

I flopped into her arms and didn't even care that I was still grassy from the outfield and wet from the sprinklers, or that a cold bottle of lemonade was giving me goosebumps where she pressed it into the back of my arm. She was easy to melt into, and just like when Franklin danced with her under the stars in the infield, she rocked me back and forth and just let me be for a minute.

"What do you think of this color, Sugar Sue?" June pulled away and smacked her lips, and all of the years between my eleven and her many more slipped away.

"Fancy, June — perfect for the first game day of the summer," I said. "It's almost even the Rock-skipper red."

I never talked about lipstick with Garland and Triple. Color only mattered to them when the gas gauge got to red or the evergreens weren't so green.

"There's this new one you might like — it's called Christmas Nutmeg. Doesn't make much sense to smear Christmas Nutmeg on your lips when it's hotter than the devil's sauna here in Ridge Creek, but it sure is beautiful."

And that was the first time I ever thought the name Derby Christmas Clark was glamorous like hers.

"It's gonna be a fine summer, Sugar Sue." June disappeared into her box office. She didn't come back out with strawberries or oatmeal raisin cookies like she did when we were on her porch, but she did have two old Rockskippers seat cushions. It looked like the cush part had long gone, but we plopped onto them, right on the front steps of the stadium.

"Did you get in real late?" she asked.

"Not too bad," I said. "After it'd gotten dark, but we still did the ride-around."

June sipped her lemonade, which left a little ring of red around the rim of the bottle. "Lots to see, hmm?"

"I mean, it would be impossible to get the Rambler down by the creek, so we didn't get there yet," I said. "Triple's already down there, of course."

"Because of Charlie?"

She was right about that. Charlie Bell was the littlest daughter of one of the pitchers, and she always won the turtle race at the Rally. I'd always told Triple not to get so hung up on those dumb turtles, because she had twelve whole months to train them in Ridge Creek, and Triple was stuck with not even one.

"I suppose Mr. Bell wasn't traded during the off-season?" I asked hopefully. June laughed the kind where you throw your center of gravity out of whack, and I could have sworn I saw her tear up a little too. I wasn't sure what was so funny.

"How's Marcus?" I continued.

"Marcus?" June got that faraway look again, but this time it came with a smile. "Bet he's one of the greatest friends you'll ever count on. Been looking forward to this day all spring too, you know."

"Opening Day?" I blew across the top of my lemonade bottle, making a sound low and slow like June's own song.

"I mean the day you get back here — that's the one he's been looking forward to, Derby."

"Oh." I didn't want to rush away my time with June, but it was nice to know that someone was counting on my rambling just as much as I was counting on their solid ground.

"Do you and Triple want behind-the-dugout seats again? Every game? I haven't sold those yet, see, because I knew you were coming," June said. "How about Garland? Can we make it three this year?"

I couldn't remember a time that Garland had taken me to a Rockskippers game. He always worried about the Grill and the burgers and the mustard tubs, and even on the night the Rockskippers' marquee shouted **CHRISTMAS IN JULY! GET YOUR STADIUM IN A SNOWGLOBE!** he didn't show up.

Maybe baseball just wasn't his sport.

"I'll ask him, June," I said. "But I'm pretty sure he's as close as he's gonna get to the bleachers right now."

"Well, then. Two it is."

"Two it is," I said. "Speaking of two, how's Franklin? I didn't see him when I snuck in."

June set down her lemonade bottle and put her chin in her hands. "Franklin," she said, and left it at that, because just then someone shuffled down the stairs. Ferdie carried a big box that must have held the letters for the marquee, because he'd dropped one or two behind him. June creaked her way to standing, picking up an *L* and a *P* along the way.

"Excuse me, ladies," Ferdie said. "I've just got to finish this up before this afternoon."

"Excuse me, too," I said. "I think it's about time for me to find Marcus at the creek." I picked up both of the lemonade bottles so Ferdie wouldn't have to, and skipped down the steps toward the Rambler's side of the parking lot.

"See you both for batting practice!" I said, and off I went.

Six

WHEN I ran through the parking lot where the Rambler sat still, Garland was fixing up the Christmas lights and the ribbons and the greenery around the Grill. I slowed down enough for the trotting kind of high-five, even though it sounded like he wanted me to stay awhile.

"Derby," I heard him say.

"The creek!" I said back, and kept going.

But before I could get all the way to the creek, I heard my stomach grumble. Since I hadn't eaten eggs with Triple and hadn't eaten strawberries and oatmeal raisin cookies with June, I was awful hungry. Maybe I should have stopped at the Grill after all, but the Sweet Street Mart wasn't such a bad pit stop instead. After all, they'd been filling bellies and hearts since 1957.

Only problem was, that's where Betsy Plogger spent her time. She didn't like the creek so much, since she was fussy about her hair and things, so the air-conditioned pickle-smell of *Sweet Street* was how she stayed cool and kept track of Ridge Creek's business.

And so of course when I got close, I saw both of those Ploggers right outside: Betsy and Lollie. They were the only two girl cousins in the whole Plogger bunch, and so Lollie was the only one who ever paid any attention to Betsy. Lollie was a year younger than me, so I didn't pay her much attention either. Betsy, though, was one year older and a full head shorter, and she ran around Ridge Creek like the boss of everybody.

Nobody knew where Betsy's mother was. Sometimes I wondered if that's why Betsy was so mean-hearted, but then I figured it must be something else, because nobody knew where my mama was either and I didn't go around trying to be the boss of everybody.

I flattened my hair down with my fingers and hoped I didn't smell too much like a cheeseburger. "Hey, Betsy. Lollie." I also hoped I was faking nice enough that they couldn't tell I was gritting my teeth.

Betsy twirled around Sweet Street's front porch banisters, and Lollie copied her. Both smacked their gum like cud-chewing cows, and Betsy blew three whole bubbles before she said hello.

"Welcome back to another summer of flipping burgers, Derby," she said. "You might lose a whole lot of money this summer. I became a vegetarian." The way she strung out *vegetaaaaaaaaarian* into a ten-second word made me forget I was trying to hide my teeth-gritting.

"That's real nice, Betsy, but the Rockskippers are a pretty hungry bunch of boys, so I'm not too worried about one twelve-year-old *vegetaaaaaaaaarian*." I couldn't help it. I'm pretty sure Lollie wanted to laugh. "Well, if *you* still eat burgers, Lollie, it's two-for-one Wednesdays again this summer. And Garland's making some new sweet-potato fries that I learned about somewhere down in Mississippi."

Betsy rolled her eyes and blew a fourth and fifth bubble.

"That's kind of like eating your vegetables and dessert at the same time," said Lollie, looking between me and Betsy for some kind of nod.

Number six popped loudly.

"I guess so," I said back, sort of disgusted by Betsy's deflated bubble.

"Do you still have real dessert too, like ice cream or something?" Lollie asked.

"Sure," I said. "Sprinkles and everything."

With one fierce glare from Betsy, the nice parts of Lollie got sucked back inside, and that was the last I'd hear from her for a while.

Then Betsy turned that glare to me. "I guess you'll be using the lobby bathroom again this summer?"

Pop.

Pop.

"I guess so," I said. "Good thing Lollie's got a real nice mom."

And I did mean that about Candy Plogger, for Lollie's sake. But if Betsy was anything like me, it would sting. Even still, spitting out that kind of thing made me not so hungry anymore, so I figured it was time to go see about Marcus.

"See you later, Ploggers. And don't forget, sweet-potato fries — they're even *vegetaaaaaaaaaarian!*"

Good thing I had turned around by that point, because if I had gritted my teeth any harder, they would have shoved themselves up into my brain.

Seven

RIGHT when I'd untangled my heart from that conversation, I had to do the same with the vines of honeysuckle to get to the creek. Betsy would never fight this sweet wall just to get to the water, but she was really missing out. Not that I was ever missing her, but still.

Something familiar was on the ground, small and blue. It was a rubber band, and I figured it had snapped off Twang. Triple had barely known our mother; he didn't even have two years with her before she was gone. But Twang was built out of a shoebox that had held her favorite sandals, and it was about all Triple had of her.

He probably hadn't even noticed that his blue string was missing, on account of the turtles on his brain. But I scooped it up and stuck it in my pocket, figuring I'd come to the rescue of a shoebox banjo that used to hold sandals.

And that's when I felt it. A small tube, cool and compact, with a tiny circle sticker on one end.

June.

She must have slipped the Christmas Nutmeg into my pocket while we were having lemonades under the marquee. That made me do the kind of grin where you put your hand over your mouth and you don't even realize it went there. But I stuck the lipstick back in my pocket real quick, 'cause I didn't want to lose it to the quick-moving waters of Ridge Creek itself.

The path to the creek was well marked, thanks to all of the running back and forth kids had done here since who knew how long ago. You had to be careful in some spots or you'd get a branch in the face, but even after being gone for a year, I knew right where to leap and right where to duck. And after I'd gone about the distance around the bases, there it was.

Triple was a few rocks away, face-down near the small rapids and the muck.

"Hey, Triple!" I yelled. "Any luck?"

All I got back was a halfhearted wave, and I couldn't tell if that was good news or bad. So I flopped down on a rock, careful to keep my sneakers out of soaking distance. And then I twisted up the Christmas Nutmeg, rich and smooth and beautiful, and I put it on the best I knew how. That's why I didn't notice at first when Marcus showed up.

"Derby, what the heck is all that paint you're putting on your face?"

"And why are you so filthy?" He had red dirt all over, from his knees down to his feet and from his elbows out to his hands.

Neither one of us was mad, of course — sometimes it's easier to pick on a friend than to just say hello. And then we smiled and did our most favorite version of a Rockskippers victory high-five, one we had studied for two-thirds of a season before we got it right, the one that went *right slap, left slap, right slap, fake the left slap and tap shoulders twice instead, slap the back of your left hands, go down low for a five on the right and then snap your way out.*

By the time the snaps were through, a whole year had fizzled away.

"How's June?" Marcus asked, a little quiet. "You saw her?"

"June? Great, I think. She said it's going to be a fine summer," I said. "Oh shoot, I forgot to tell her about the sweet-potato fries. You are going to love them with a burger or two. Unless you became a vegetarian since last year."

"What?" Marcus flipped his wilder-this-summer hair around a little, and then said, "Oh. Betsy."

"Oh, Betsy," I said, and then our smiles turned to the laughing kind.

Through the trees shading the creek, we could hear Miss Houston's kerplunks. She was the organist at the stadium, and she wasn't all that good. But that meant batting practice was close, and watching the warm-ups was what Marcus and I always did on game days. We'd stand low in the bleachers pretty close to the bullpen and watch his dad, Lump Emmett, shag balls and joke around with the rest of the outfield. The rest of that outfield happened to be Goose and Scooter Plogger, who played right and center field alongside Lump's left, and they happened to be Lollie's dad and Betsy's dad. Lollie and Betsy weren't into batting practice like we were.

"Derby," Marcus said, "I gotta go. I can't make batting practice." And before I could even ask him why or why not or anything at all, he leaped and ducked his way away from the creek.

"Marcus Emmett, get back here! It's tradition!"

I hoped a root would stub his toe and slow him down, but it didn't. He was gone.

And so was Triple. I'd probably have to do the onions.

Eight

I FOUGHT my way back through the honeysuckle, which seemed to hang lower than it had on my way in. Once the mud on the path had turned back to dirt, both Marcus's and Triple's footprints disappeared. But each step took me closer to where they were supposed to be, toward the stop-and-start of Miss Houston's notes, toward the hit-and-run of the Rockskippers' warm-ups.

Back at the stadium, I stopped behind FILLING and BELLIES and pressed my face as close to the bow in the boards as I could without being in danger of splinters. There was no shimmying through when the Rockskippers had the field, since a fly ball was way more dangerous than a sliver of wood. And at that angle, I couldn't even see our spot close to the dugout. That was where I was supposed to be with Triple in one hour, watching Marcus roaming around somewhere nearby.

It was my opening day in Ridge Creek.

And now it was all wrong.

What in the world was going on with Marcus Emmett? Sneaking around the same way Garland did when there was pie involved? Running off to who-knew-where and not even telling me?

At least there's always June, I thought. *I should thank her for the Christmas Nutmeg.* I circled around the long way, behind left field to the front of the stadium, avoiding the Grill side of the parking lot because maybe Triple had gone back and been stuck with the onions and would holler at me for help.

The stadium was a bit more bustling now. Season regulars dotted that side of the parking lot, wishing and hoping and praying for their boys. That meant, of course, that June was already in business at the box office.

I was kind of invisible in that field of folks, but I could still soak in whatever it was they were whispering to each other. All of their eyes looked up more than at each other, and mine searched for what they were looking at.

Up there on the marquee were the rest of Ferdie's letters.

SAVE US ALL A DANCE, FRANKLIN MATTINGLY.
THE ROCKSKIPPERS MISS YOU.

Save.

I stared at that marquee so long that the insides of my eyelids saw fuzzy spots, soft and gray and angry all at once. Those things under my eyelids moved down to my belly, almost like the sinking feeling was the news itself, soaking into each bone, slow and sure.

"Derby," I heard from somewhere out of reach.

For the second time that day, June hugged me. And it should have been the other way around, me making posters for her and hugging her and bringing her ice-cold lemonades. Maybe that's why she hadn't wanted to be on her front porch, with the swinging and the strawberries. Maybe that's why we'd met at the box office. Maybe being close to his name on the marquee stuck her extra tight to him.

"June," I said. "How? Why?"

She held my face in her hands, like an expert in the art of comfort. "It was time, Derby. He got sick, and it went fast, and we sent him to forever with some dirt from this place." She waved her arm toward the stadium when she said that, toward the place they both called home. "The man at the funeral home thought that was real strange, but I knew Franklin would be right understanding of all that dirt."

"I wish I had known," I said.

"We had his service right here, right on the field."

"I bet you were awful careful with his grass?"

"Sure were," June said. "He'd have been gnawing at his fingernails if he knew about all those feet on his turf, but I bet he wouldn't have wanted it any other way."

"He knew," I said.

"I know," she said.

The line was getting longer at June's box office, wrapping into the parking lot where some kids were playing catch, but nobody mentioned the waiting. They let her be and let me be, and we stood there under Franklin's name until batting practice was nearly over and I was real late for prep at the Grill.

Nine

GARLAND always said aren't we lucky, 'cause whether the creek rises or the pit sinks, we'd just ramble on to the next pin in the map. Leapfrogging those pins made me homesick, but I guess there could still be heartache even when your pin was planted in one place.

I walked real slow from the stadium to our side of the parking lot, hoping to get a little distance from the marquee. Except that wasn't any kind of possible, what with the Grill being only one long sweet-potato-fries line away.

There Garland was, sitting on the step to the Rambler and unraveling the last of the Christmas-tree lights for the Grill. Maybe he'd been waiting for me. Maybe he'd seen the marquee too.

"Hey, Garland," I said, scooting in next to him on the step.

Garland wrapped his arm around me and said, "How's June?"

That's when I finally cried the kind of cry where your breath catches up in your throat and you can't suck in a good one without your shoulders rising up. He didn't say anything, but he didn't let me go.

"Did you know?" I asked him.

"Candy Plogger sent me a message at Christmastime. Right about when things are supposed to be the happiest. I didn't want to wreck things for you and your brother."

Garland hated the idea of troubles interrupting such a jolly time. We must have been wrapping trees like huge burritos right about then, watching the white lights coming and the red lights going. And here was June Mattingly, left alone like the bright North Star itself.

"She said this was gonna be a fine summer," I said.

"Could still be," Garland said. "She's got you back. That makes her awful lucky."

"Can you come to the game? She asked if you'd be there."

Garland fidgeted with his lights, knotting them

up even more than they'd been when he started. "No, ma'am," he said. "Not my thing."

"I'm sorry I missed prep time. Tell Triple I'll clean up extra for him tonight."

"Not my thing," he said once more, quieter.

I'd heard him, though, so I stood up to wash the dirt and tears off and let him finish that untangling all by himself. Another trip to the Heritage Inn wasn't real high on my want-to-do list, but it was necessary, and so I went.

"Did you fall in the creek or what?" Of course Betsy saw me. Lollie was with her, matching step for step.

"The *or what* part," I said.

I wasn't in the mood for trading eyerolls with Betsy Plogger. I kind of just wanted to go to the bathroom and get on with things. The two of them marched past, leaving behind poofs of more perfume than any girl had business putting on.

"See you at the game?" Lollie said, letting Betsy get a step ahead of her.

I could have sworn she even smiled at me a little.

Ten

TRIPLE, are you ready? Come on, it's time."

He was still dirty from the onions and whatever else he'd prepped at the Grill, but making him clean himself up wasn't worth a rumble.

"Charlie said it's twenty-five whole dollars for the winner this year. That's five more than last summer!" Triple stuck a pickle spear toward a turtle's mouth. Twang wasn't doing much good as a banjo anymore, because he'd taken up a new job as a turtle habitat.

"Looks like a fast one," I said, whether or not I believed it. "What's his name?"

Triple thought for a minute. "Peter," he said. And then he ate the pickle spear himself.

"Peter. Okay, then," I said. At least someone around here had a good old-fashioned normal name.

"Ready?" Triple asked me that question like I hadn't asked him first, as though he'd gotten transfixed by Peter and a pickle and forgotten that the first game was about to start.

But I laughed, and I didn't argue when Triple said he was bringing Peter along. Sometimes, later in the summer, the marquee read **BRING YOUR DOG TO THE STADIUM DAY! BEER FOR YOU! BONES FOR THEM!** And so if Ferdie was okay with a bunch of drooling dogs, I'm sure he'd be okay with a turtle in a shoebox.

"You really don't want to come, Garland?" I knew the answer would still be no, but it's like he always said — food, family, and fun. Asking again was the family part of that.

The look on his face was all the answer I needed. It looked a little sad, like when you hear some music that stirs up something inside your soul that you didn't even know was there.

"Okay," I said. "We'll see you after."

"I'll leave the light on for you — all three thousand of them!" And there it was again, the sparkle that made Garland Garland.

We didn't need to wait in June's box-office line. She'd given me the tickets already, and the fewer people who had to meet Peter, the better.

Triple and I always sat together behind the

dugout on the first-base side — every inning, every out, every game. I liked having some time with just him, and I think he liked it too. Marcus was always nearby, but he was more of a roamer, so once our batting-practice routine would end, we'd high-five goodbye until the sun set and the burgers flipped. He liked left field to give Lump a little oomph and he liked close behind home plate to taunt the ump. But a lot of the time he'd just get bored with baseball and sneak into the bullpen to share some pistachios and blow bubbles with the relievers.

Even though he was supposed to be everywhere, Marcus wasn't anywhere. And I was still mad at him for not telling me why.

As Triple and I scrambled up the steps and the noise of the stadium tickled my bones, I felt like a small part of something big. Miss Houston whaled on the organ with all the dazzle of a third-base coach wildly waving a runner home. Rockskippers were scattered on the field in their blue-and-whites while they stretched and spat and scratched. Howls of "Peanuts! Popcorn! Cotton can-day!" echoed from the upper deck.

Triple seemed less enchanted by the magic that

was swirling around and much more interested in the *cotton can-day.*

"Fine, fine, Triple. Let's just sit down first."

Charlie Bell's dad was pitching. I liked him an extra bunch because we were both lefties. When he ran out to take the mound, he flashed me a thumbs-up, the left one.

"Strikes, Mr. Bell!" I yelled down to the field. "And, hey, free sweet-potato fries all summer for the first shutout!"

Garland might not have been too thrilled by my giving away free sweet-potato fries, but that was how easy it was to get caught up in the glory of this old place. Even Peter was clambering all around inside Twang with the most excitement a turtle could muster.

"This is awesome," said Triple.

"Yeah," I said.

It was.

And it still was through the first four innings. The outfielders ran all around the grass out there, protecting their turf from the other guys' runs. Mr. Bell threw more strikes than balls, and the newest Rockskipper even hit a home run.

But then the fifth inning came around, and the stadium roar lowered to a hush. Everyone waited. Everyone wondered.

"Where's Franklin?" Triple asked.

What about June? I thought.

Lump Emmett caught an easy fly ball to end the top of the inning. I'm pretty sure he also caught flickers of memories in his glove, because he stood still for just a nod and a beat before jogging back toward the dugout. I looked around for Marcus, sure he would be raising his fists in pride and jumping higher than the rest of the crowd.

I still didn't see him anywhere.

Miss Houston began to play, and her song had hints of bittersweet vibrating through it. Maybe I was the only one hearing things, but one ear heard a rousing in-between-innings tune and the other heard heartbreak.

But the Rockskippers didn't go into the dugout for the switch. Instead, clump by clump of brawny ballplayers stood guard just outside the bullpen, which wasn't much more than some dirt and overturned buckets for chairs just across the foul line from shallow right field.

It's also where Franklin Mattingly had kept his rakes and tools and cart. And there was June Mattingly, in the bullpen without him.

Clump by clump, the Rockskippers took off their ball caps, revealing bald heads, sweat-soaked hair, and a whole lot of awkward smiles that stretched more down than up.

June stood still. She smiled back, hers a little more successful in the upward way.

"Is that Miss June?" Triple had to stand on his seat to see.

I didn't answer. Because then, introduced by a few clunky plunks from Miss Houston, the ramshackle bullpen fence swung open and out came Franklin Mattingly's cart.

Marcus was driving it.

Even from all the way behind the dugout I could tell how fiercely he was gripping the steering wheel, knuckles whiter than a brand-new baseball. When he got to the infield, he hopped out, unfurled the rake, and moved through the motions of groundskeeping, swift and fluid.

I held my breath when he rounded second base — and I think the whole stadium did too. But Marcus didn't dance. He only raked and patted and dragged in a kind of businesslike manner. And it didn't really matter if I watched Marcus or June or the army of Rockskippers, because my eyes blurred and burned anyway.

Back at the bullpen, June wrapped her arms around Marcus.

And then the Rockskippers put their caps back on, Miss Houston plunked an oops or two, and the game continued like it was just another hot Ridge Creek evening, the sun dropping over the James Edward Allen Gibbs Stadium.

Eleven

OPENING Day for the Rockskippers meant Opening Night for Garland's Grill, so all of Ridge Creek tumbled out into our side of the parking lot for cheeseburgers and play-by-playing after the game. The Rockskippers had won, 4–1, which meant it'd be as crowded as the creek on a blazing day. Everyone had room for snacks and chatter when we were the champs. And even though I was happy about my fellow southpaw's win, I was happier that I wouldn't have to sneak him any free shutout sweet-potato fries just yet.

Garland made Triple wash up real good and leave Peter in the Rambler, and even though I didn't think he'd want to find Peter relaxing in the kitchenette's sink, it was where that turtle was. Triple turned Twang back into an instrument, since Peter had a place to hang out for a while, and that's when I remembered the blue rubber band.

"Here," I said, and flicked it in his direction.

And because it was also in my pocket, I sweetened myself up a touch with the Christmas Nutmeg and splashed some water on my face before we left the Rambler.

"Hey!" Triple said. "Peter!"

"Easy, Triple. He's probably used to being wet."

The two of us walked to the Grill, which took about as much time as a bowling ball takes to split the pins. Triple did his acoustic act up and down the line and I ducked inside to help Garland. Even though Triple was a small thing, only two Clarks fit inside the Grill if you didn't want an elbow in your side. I flung orders and Garland flipped burgers, and while I stacked the baskets, he steamed the buns. All of his *Aren't we luckys* vibrated real loud in my ears, and I tried not to sweat all over the sweet-potato fries. We'd perfected this cramped choreography of the Grill long ago, so I stepped in time as best I could.

"Southpaw!"

Mr. Bell's untied sneakers were the only thing I could see, so I bent down to catch a better picture through the tiny pickup window, grateful to suck in real Ridge Creek air instead of the steamy onion sauna of the Grill. And then I stuck out my left thumb.

"Real nice stuff out there, Mr. Bell! Bummer about that line drive Lump missed, or else I'd be fixing you a bunch of sweet-potato fries, right?"

"Well, the season's young, young'un!"

The way he pitched right back to me made Charlie laugh a little. She'd been hiding behind him like she was shy, even though Triple always made her sound bossy and too much like Betsy Plogger for her own good. I snuck a smile at her anyway.

"Three cheeseburgers and three sweet potato fries, and that'll be all," he said. "And does your banjo man out here take requests?"

"He's a little light on variety, but you can try." Talking about Triple like that turned Charlie's shy to smug real quick, so maybe he wasn't too far off about her after all.

But then the line shifted and I wished I hadn't blamed Lump Emmett for wrecking the shutout. Because there was Marcus, right behind Charlie and her daddy that whole time.

He stared at me and I stared back, and my mouth kind of froze in the *I want to say something* way, but nothing came out. He didn't call me a flycatcher or anything, so I bet he was just as stuck on words as I was. And Garland bumped my hip, reminding me that I had broken time in our tune.

Then Marcus laughed.

So did I.

And we were back.

"Hungry?" I asked, knowing the answer. "So, grounds crew? You should've told me."

"Starving. All they've got in the bullpen is pistachios and chewing tobacco, and that stuff will rust up your teeth."

"And your mom would have a fit, right?" I wrote up a ticket for Marcus's favorite — two hamburgers with extra mustard, extra pickles, and stuffed with onion rings — and reached it over to Garland.

Garland swung around. "No way this order belongs to anyone besides my man Marcus Emmett!"

"Hey, Garland," Marcus said. "Welcome back."

"How's your mother?"

"Real good. She's real good. Says she's been perfecting a new pie recipe for the Rally, if you'll be there."

"Well, of course," Garland said. "The best kind of food is the dessert kind, right?"

He never said anything about the Rally being fun, but he was real into the food. That's probably because the Rally had every kind of pie anyone could ever imagine, and Garland was pretty good at imagining. The best-tasting baked thing won a ribbon and bragging rights for the whole next year, and the Ridge Creek ladies thought that was better than any kind of pennant. Last year Estelle Hooch's chocolate chip cookies beat out every single one of the pies, including Candy Plogger's Famous Apple. Candy didn't take that too well, but those cookies were even better than June's.

All the Rockskippers skipped warm-ups and batting practice on Rally Day and let kids try to knock them into the dunk tank or smack water balloons into the backs of their jerseys, right in the numbers. It was a way for all of Ridge Creek to feel like a Rockskipper for a day, and the players were real good sports about it, even if they didn't play too well later on account of all those pies.

Garland couldn't wait for the pies, and Triple was even more excited, since the Rally was when the turtle race happened. The whole day was kind of like a church potluck, but without the church and with a lot more reptiles. It was mostly in the stadium parking lot, but some parts stretched to the inside, like the race-around-the-bases and the kids' softball game. With an actual game later, it was a real busy day for the grounds crew, who'd always been a crew of just one.

"The Rally. Big day for you now," I said down to Marcus once Garland twirled back around to the burgers.

"I know." And then Marcus bent down and picked up a penny.

"This year?" I strained to see if it was shiny in his palm. Marcus looked up at me and smiled, which was a loud and clear yes.

"See you there," I said. I handed Marcus his two hamburgers with extra mustard, extra pickles, and stuffed with onion rings, and off he went.

Remembering Marcus on Franklin's cart was like catching the faintest glimpse of myself. I wondered if I would help at the box office if it were June who was gone — and what about the rest of the year? Had anyone sat with her on the porch eating oatmeal raisin cookies since Christmastime? My gut sank lower, right to the spot where sadness goes.

It struck my brain then that I didn't really know much about June Mattingly through the other seasons. She'd been here for me, summer after summer after summer, but I'd only ever offered her endless burgers and fries in return.

"Derby? Hello? A milkshake?" And as quick and quiet as those thoughts had come, they floated away like the swirls of a just-blown-out candle, because Betsy was next in line.

"Sure. A nice *vegetarian* option, of course," I said.

With a Triple and Twang tune in my head — something about racing turtles and turtledoves — the rest of the short night in the Grill seemed like it was exactly what Garland loved: food, family, and fun. But my heart jumped along with the grease splatters when I thought about the *Aren't we lucky* part.

I didn't think we were very lucky at all. Lucky is having one good girl cousin and vegetarian french fries. All we were was tired and sad and smelling like onions.

Twelve

LATER that night, Garland was at our teensy kitchen table, scattering cookie crumbs and sipping his nightly chamomile tea in his favorite mug — the one with a picture of Santa Claus chopping down a snowy Christmas tree. He and Triple always fought over it, because Santa Claus's pants were ripped and you could see right through to his snowflake-patterned underpants.

Peter was traipsing around on the floorboards, which startled me a notch, and so when I fell onto the bench alongside Garland, I almost spilled Santa Claus and his unmentionables.

"Triple —" I said, catching my breath and the mug. And then I saw the dollar bills stacked in neat piles, all across the table.

"Derby Christmas Clark, it's the sweet-potato fries! That must be what people love, the sweet-potato fries—" Garland sputtered on like a mad scientist admiring his monster. "I don't think we've ever been tipped this good on an Opening Night!"

"Here's a tip," said Triple, crawling around behind Peter. "Don't feed your turtle something he might mix up with a finger." Triple had Band-Aids on about three of his, so he must have been speaking from experience.

"At least that's not your strumming hand," I said.

Garland hummed something mumble-like and Triple did too, and I was the only rambler without a song.

"When you said to turn those tubers into fries, I really didn't believe you, Derby. I mean, vegetables other than onions? At Garland's Grill? Seems like it would work for Triple or Charlie Bell or someone who is still learning the ropes in this world, but grown people? Fried-up vegetables?"

Garland kissed my head, but it felt a little like he used my hair as a napkin for his crumbs. And then he paced away, up toward the driver's seat, his hands each clutching a fistful of dollars. Right behind the reclining part was the safe where we kept important things — things like our money, the papers that let us operate the Grill, and Twang's new just-in-case strings. Garland would rip out recipes from magazines we found at truck stops along the way and stick them in too, just in case he ever felt like making rotisserie chicken and zucchini frittatas and roasted peaches with caramel sauce.

He never did.

I'd known the code since long ago, the summer everything changed for us. Garland said as the lady of the place I'd get to know the important things, and the code was one of them. It was 0621, the last day my mama was a rambler, and that became the key to everything we kept safe. Maybe she meant to make the longest day of the year her last day with us, so that every June 21 after, some extra daylight meant more time we couldn't see her.

I really hoped she hadn't, but it's what I wonder every single year.

When the night was ending and the boys in the Rambler were about to count sheep, I got ready to finish the last thing of my first day back in Ridge Creek. It was easy to forgive Marcus for skipping out on batting practice, because of the fifth inning and all, but he knew I'd spit on his onion rings if he missed meeting at the marquee.

But first I stuck Peter back into the sink so Garland wouldn't step on him. Triple had sunk into the sticky plastic sofa, a matted mess of sweat and sunscreen, not even making it to his bunk. He was in that fuzzy place between sleep and serious, Twang in his hands.

"Night, Derby," he said, full of sweet. "Teach me a high-five soon?"

"Tomorrow. First thing." It was a whisper and a promise. "Rockskipper high-five and turtle training."

A quick change and a little Christmas Nutmeg later, I headed out to the stadium. I didn't need to worry about being too quiet — both Triple and Garland sawed logs in their sleep.

I think it reminded them of the Christmas trees.

Thirteen

MARCUS beat me to the marquee.

There he was, sitting right under it and shaking the last ice cubes in his soda cup from the Grill. I didn't say anything—not because I was trying to creep up on him, but because I didn't have the right words anyway.

Instead, I grabbed his other hand, pulled him up, and started our favorite Rockskipper high-five whether he wanted to or not. By the time we got to the shoulder-tap part, we'd both found some words.

"What's up with the lipstick?" Marcus asked, and even though I wished he'd found something different to say, it sounded nicer than what he'd said about my face at the creek.

"June gave it to me." I pressed my lips together, not entirely sure if I thought I was fixing the Christmas Nutmeg or hiding it.

"Is she gonna give you a hairbrush one of these days?"

I could see all over his face that he was teasing, but since he didn't understand a single thing about being glamorous, I shoved him on the last shoulder I'd tapped.

"Help! Please! My raking arm—" He taunted right back with a real pathetic fake groan. The combination of me trying not to let him see me laugh and his fake stumbles sent us both into fits. And when Marcus collapsed once more underneath those marquee letters, I sat down right next to him on the concrete steps.

"Ferdie already changed the sign." Marcus looked down.

"Oh." I made myself look up, and tried to hide the shake in my own voice. "'Sunglasses Tuesday! Sport Rockskipper Shades!'"

Marcus took a big sip of nothing from his empty cup.

"That's—real important," I said. "You know, with how dangerous the sun is these days and all."

I couldn't figure out the look Marcus gave me.

But then, quiet as a whisper with laryngitis, he said: *Franklin.*

I knew then that his look was a kind of flood wall, holding back the choppy waters of sorrow and hope and boys-don't-cry. So I put my hand on top of his. It took a while for his shoulders to stop shaking, and when they did, his face was still red-hot with leftover tears.

"You're his Sugar Sue?" As soon as I asked that question, I knew it sounded ridiculous, but I was still so startled by his storm.

"I'm his Skipper. He calls me that. Well, *called* me. This year, while you were out rambling."

I studied his face, threw time in reverse, and tried to see what I had missed. "So, the grounds crew? That's why you couldn't watch batting practice with me like always? You'd rather dig around in the dirt than watch the boys knock homers on it?"

"Derby, I don't want to play that old ball. You know how my dad's been forever and always — thinking I'm some mini-Lump, ready to drop in and take over left field the second he gets a head full of grays."

"You love baseball," I said, trying to understand.

"Yeah, yeah, I do. But I figured out that I don't want to play it. Goose and Scooter probably aren't having those same conversations my dad is with me, because Betsy and Lollie are just girls. I mean, not that I wish I was one of them, but at least they *can't* play ball. For me, it's like there's not even a choice."

Marcus's unwinding threw me a bit off-balance, but that girl part still stung. He kept on. "What would Garland say if you told him you hate Christmas trees and flipping burgers? Wouldn't he leave you right on the side of the road?" Marcus threw his cup to the ground, and it rolled back and forth before it settled down.

After that, it was quiet. But since friends know the different kinds of quiets, I waited for him. I didn't think he was actually expecting an answer to that last question anyway, seeing as that was pretty much what my mama had done.

"Sorry about the girl thing. And the side-of-the-road thing," Marcus said. "I didn't mean it."

"I know."

"Ferdie caught me after Franklin was gone, Lefty," Marcus said, riding a wave of relief. "Poking around in the bullpen. At first I thought he was afraid I was gonna raid the fertilizer stash or something, but then I figured him out a little."

Marcus said it with all the seriousness of Miss Houston's organ-playing hopes, but I couldn't suck the chuckle in fast enough. "Marcus Emmett: The Baseline Lime Looter!"

He shot me a look that would freeze an August creek, but I knew he thought it was funny. "Ferdie's not so strange, you know. Stood next to June at Franklin's service. Patted her shoulder and handed her tissues every once in a while."

"I've never seen him that friendly with anyone," I said, looking up at the marquee. Those letters tonight seemed so silly for someone with such a quiet way about him.

"I know. And so he told me that Franklin wouldn't have wanted me just poking around, and he gave me the keys to the mower. Haven't lost them yet." Marcus patted his pocket and it gave a little jingle. "He's even paying me a little bit of money, but I'd have done it anyway."

"For Franklin," I said.

"For Franklin," he echoed.

It wasn't like I didn't know and love Franklin

Mattingly like the rest of Ridge Creek did, but I didn't remember him and Marcus having much of anything in common besides the Rockskippers. Maybe my friendship with June had gotten in the way of realizing other people might be looking for someone to share lemonades with.

"It started over Thanksgiving," Marcus continued, as if he'd heard me wondering. "My dad and I went over to the stadium with Goose and Scooter. We had to throw balls and run off some pie, and my dad thought that was why I was all weird."

"Weird?"

"Yeah, like I'd had one too many pieces of chocolate chiffon and the sugar had made me grumpy or something."

Turns out, the grumping was because Marcus didn't want to play that old ball. Not one bit. And he let his dad know.

Marcus said Lump was so mad that he left his best glove right there in the outfield. And Marcus said *he* was so mad that he just stayed there, with Lump's best glove. When the sun dropped and the chill rose, Marcus moved to the bullpen and fell asleep under Franklin Mattingly's tarp.

"How did you make it under there, sleeping in the cold all night?" I knew Ridge Creek never got to be Wisconsin cold, but I never would have thought Marcus's stubbornness would be bigger than his comfort. It made me awful sad, though — the thought of only that tarp protecting Marcus, as if he were just plain old dirt and grass.

"I mean, I was mad, but my dad was right about having one too many pieces of chocolate chiffon," he said. "That sugar knocked me out cold as the weather."

Bright and early the next morning, when Thanksgiving had barely turned into a regular old day, Franklin had found him.

"Ah, the Skipper awakes," Franklin had said.

Marcus said he was a jumble of apologies and embarrassment and the shivers, but Franklin didn't seem to see any of that. It was like he'd been waiting for him, for who knows how long.

And from then on, Marcus was just the Skipper, wrapped up into Franklin's fold. Neither one of them would know they'd only have a month together.

"Hey," Marcus said. "We almost forgot."

He dug into his pocket, the one that jingled with

the groundskeeper's keys, and pulled out the penny from earlier. I inspected the date to make sure our luck might work, and we placed the coin right between our thumbs. When we were little, Lump had told us that if you found a penny that matched the year, you could make a wish that would come true by the close of summer. He said the James Edward Allen Gibbs Stadium was as good as any old pool of water, and so each year after that, we'd wished on as many new pennies as we found, thinking Lump was as reliable as the heat. As we got older, I figured we were just leaving pennies in the bleachers for Ferdie to have to clean up, but maybe he needed a little bit of luck too.

Garland never did like me digging through the tip jars, so it was a good thing that Marcus had found this one on the ground. I don't know if we broke the rules by sharing a penny and not our wishes, but it was the way it was.

After the wishing, Marcus and I sat under the shouts of **SUNGLASSES TUESDAY!** until I was pretty sure we saw the stars shift. We crossed the parking lot once more, me toward the Rambler and him toward home.

I didn't tell Marcus, but I'd wished on June her-self. Why had she wanted me to meet her at the box office and not her front porch? If Marcus could keep a secret, then I could too. Except this secret was just a whole bunch of *I don't know yet.*

JUNE 8

Fourteen

EVEN without a lot of luxurious sleep in my queen room, I woke up in the morning fit as a fiddle. Or in my particular case, sharp as a shoebox banjo.

I remembered the night before with Marcus, when our loud and laughing minutes had outnumbered our quiet ones, and even though I was still a teensy bit annoyed at him for spoiling my first day by ditching me at the creek, it almost felt like the summer could start fresh.

Except it couldn't.

Franklin was still gone, June was still alone, and those troubles were bigger than wishes could solve.

Triple must have already been down at the creek with Peter, and Garland was busying himself at the Grill with his chalkboard art and checking the Christmas lightbulbs. I was alone in the Rambler. I grabbed a mug from the sink—not the Santa Claus one — and hoped Peter hadn't crawled all over it in the night. Just to be safe I gave it a good rinse, and poured myself the rest of the cold coffee Garland had left. And then I got dressed and put on my Christmas Nutmeg, and off I went.

I ran quick past the Grill in case Garland decided he needed help right then with the tinsel, and ran straight to June's box office. It was early still, so I figured she wouldn't be there just yet. But the thing was, I needed her to be. And I needed to wait for her unseen, still as a pitcher right before the windup. So I crouched behind that box office somewhere by the 1981 pennants and away from the watchful eye of Ferdie.

It didn't take too long before I heard her singing, breaking up the morning's haze with pretty drops of song. "Morning, Ferdie," she called to somewhere above her, and I hoped he hadn't noticed me.

"Miss June" was the only response to her call, and I pictured tissue-sharing and sadness-bearing.

But I pushed that all aside, and once I heard the box-office door shut, I took off. Marcus said that I was the only one who ever got invited over to where the Mattinglys lived, even though I'd never been past the porch. As long as Lump had been a Rockskipper, no one knew what their real place was like. Their most-of-the-time place was the James Edward Allen Gibbs Stadium, and that was okay with the people who called Ridge Creek home. Maybe it was a perk of being a rambler on the road, but whatever it was, being invited to a porch swing to sort of call your own was something special.

By invitation or not, getting there only took the time to sing the national anthem twice in a row. I didn't even fancy up the notes or anything, and there I was.

June and Franklin lived at the end of a dirt driveway that started with an impeccable bed of impatiens, and the red ones formed a massive *M* in the middle of a brilliant field of white.

Except not anymore.

The white impatiens had withered down to almost nothing, like a storm had barreled through and swallowed up all the sunshine. And the *M* was long gone — only specks of sad pink were left. Queen Anne's lace crowded around the edges of the bed, and that weed stood guard and watched over the impatiens bowing back down to the earth.

At least the weed was beautiful, and had a noble kind of job.

The house was way down the winding dirt driveway, looking like it had gotten the wind knocked out of it. Vines weaved up and around the porch like they were trying to tackle the columns to the ground, and it seemed like they were winning. What had been a bed for marigolds or squash or something had so many weeds in it that even the weeds had weeds. And our porch swing, our place for lemonade and oatmeal raisin cookies and watching the morning dew dry up, hung all alone, creaking and croaking.

"Whoa." I stepped up onto the porch, careful not to crush the little white blossoms that were trying real hard to bloom around the steps.

Ridge Creek had other houses that looked like this, like the people were too busy having spaghetti or playing checkers and weren't all that interested in flower beds and porch swings. And I'd always thought that was just fine, that the inside of a home was more important than an overgrown outside — that it didn't really matter as long as you had one.

But this was unusual for June Mattingly, with her perfect makeup and freshly pressed dresses. It was like seeing her insides spilled out all over her outside — everything in shambles and an unstoppable growth of something you didn't ask for. Something that might have been sorrow.

That's when I noticed the front door, and my toenails itched to see something so familiar: a Christmas wreath, fake like our greens on the Grill, and covered in cobwebs. It was like time had stopped ticking the minute Franklin died. The greens on Garland's Grill collected a lot of dust on the road, but even those looked merrier than this mess.

And I didn't mean to break into June's house, but when my fist hit the front door with the force of something like mad, the handle jiggled and it spilled right open. And after I'd fallen through and gotten myself upright and sturdy again, there I was, standing in the front hall. I'd never really thought about why I'd never been past the porch swing, and Garland had always told me to mind my manners and be polite and so I'd never asked.

Pictures and mementos covered the walls from the ceiling to the floor. They didn't look like much to me, but if they were important enough to be nailed to a wall, then I guess that was something. We didn't have much on the walls of the Rambler, 'cause it got too dangerous when we were on the road. Sure would be nice not to shove your favorite things into a safe behind the driver's seat and get to look at your memories whenever you wanted.

I saw keys that looked like they belonged to the barn of a giant rather than the house of a human. Yellowed newspaper clippings and church bulletins were pinned up, the print too faded and small to understand what important moment was captured forever. Bunches of dried flowers hung toward the floor, petals frozen and wrapped up in red ribbons. Everything was covered with the thinnest layer of dust, not much more than the slightest whoosh of a warm breeze.

But it wasn't the things that caught my eye so much as the people. It was hard to read the faded old pictures, but I tried.

An earlier version of June smiled from behind dusty glass in a frame — the same brown skin tinted pink at the cheeks, and a smile with some earlier match to Christmas Nutmeg. But her eyes had a different kind of sparkle — familiar, but fresh.

Franklin looked like Franklin whether the picture was from last summer or last decade, whether he was riding a lawn mower or gardening at the end of his dirt driveway. He looked like Franklin whether he was dancing with June or rocking a baby girl.

That startled me — his strong, weathered hands holding something so small and fragile. June and Franklin looked at that baby girl like she was the sun and they wanted to spin around her forever.

June was a mother.

I hadn't known.

I ran out after that, slamming the door so hard that dust fluttered off the greens, but I didn't even look back to make sure the wreath stayed in place. This time I didn't worry about trampling the tiny blossoms. My bones ached with something unfixable, like they knew the clouds were coming and wanted to buckle under the pressure.

I reached the spot where the *M* was supposed to be and picked a handful of Queen Anne's lace, and that's where I stopped.

"Derby, hey."

Betsy and Lollie Plogger stood right there in front of me, right at the end of the winding dirt driveway, right by the Mattinglys' mailbox shaped like a sun.

"What are you doing here?" I was mad that they'd caught me and madder that they knew these same steps.

"This is June's house, right? My mom wanted to send her this pie," said Lollie.

"It won't fit in this mailbox, will it?" Betsy opened and closed the sun twice, shutting it much too hard each time. And then she marched down that dirt driveway, toward what June hadn't wanted even me to see.

"Oh," I said, catching up. "I'll take it to her — I'm on my way right now."

"On your way? Didn't we just see you coming *from* there?" Betsy nodded toward the house, and I was surprised she'd been so observant. "What did you do, bring her a bunch of weeds? At least we brought a pie."

"Lollie, I can take it." I tried to take the tin from her arms, but before I could, Betsy stopped.

"Well, isn't this a shame," Betsy said, with none of

the sadness I felt when I saw the same mess. "Come on, Lollie. We don't want to walk through poison ivy or whatever else might be crawling around in there."

"Here, Derby." Lollie handed me the pie. "Tell her my mama's been thinking of her."

And so I sat on the steps of June's front porch with an apple pie in my lap, watching the weeds wave around in the hot breeze, not even sure what I was waiting for. Chickadees from somewhere nearby called out a question that I didn't have the answer to. Those birds didn't know they were supposed to be anything but cheerful. But once their song was burned into my ears and the sun blazed noon, I figured it was time to go.

All that wishing the night before, and the only thing I had now was a foil pie pan about to blister my knees. Plus a whole lot more questions.

Fifteen

I LEFT the pie on the porch. The only place that made sense to go was back to the stadium, and so I slipped through FILLING and BELLIES because it was closest to the bullpen, closest to Marcus.

I could tell a real storm was on its way because the last slivers of the thick morning air didn't have anywhere to escape to, and it drew out the sweat from my face. The clouds hung low and gray and awful, like they were settling in for a story. Soon enough there'd be nothing but mugginess and noise — rowdy Rockskippers both throwing heat and complaining about it.

That *soon enough* came real quick, when the clanking and cursing and a motor that sounded less in tune than Miss Houston's bad notes interrupted the quiet.

"Marcus Theodore Williams Emmett!"

There he was, head stuck under the hood of

Franklin's cart as if it were just another day fixing up busted cars at the body shop. His arms were caked with red mud and dirt, and each clank I'd heard was Marcus kicking the cart. At least those clanks covered up the curses.

"This crusty old thing won't start up." Marcus ignored the way I'd hollered all of his names like I was his mama or something.

"Here," I said, and used all the muscle I could squeeze into my arms to lift that hood so Marcus could tinker with the guts.

"This can't happen before the second game of the season. Franklin would never . . ."

"Maybe it'll get rained out anyway." I didn't want that to happen, but it did feel like that was the type of weather that best suited our moods.

I thought about all of the mess in June's front yard, the mess that wouldn't exist if Franklin was there to take care of it, the mess that must have reminded her every time she stepped outside. And I thought about my own family's mess, the one with wheels, the one that reminded me every day that we had a table for four and were only three.

I'd been there watching Marcus try to fix that

engine for who knows how long—and that's when I remembered my promise to Triple. "The high-five," I said.

"Derby, not right now," said Marcus. "I'm kind of busy."

"No, Marcus—it's Triple. I ditched him before I even *got* to the creek." I kicked Franklin's cart myself, but it didn't feel as good as cursing might have. "Can I have some old grass clippings? Peter could use some."

"Peter?"

"It's Triple's . . . Triple's new champion turtle."

"You know, Lefty, they're not just old grass clippings. The turf industry is way more complex than some old lady's gardening club."

It was like standing in front of Franklin Mattingly himself, like he'd stood his ground right here in Marcus, right in the bullpen at the James Edward Allen Gibbs Stadium. I inhaled a deep breath of fumes and fertilizer, but before I could say anything, Marcus rambled on.

"Did you know that Carlton Bell and Javy Avelar and Samson Brickhouse all like the pitcher's mound raked differently? Did you know it matters? A turf specialist makes sure his team can play to win." Marcus stomped down on that rake. "Twisted ankles on divots in the outfield? That's on me, Derby."

"Did he teach you how to mow the creek ripples in the outfield?" I hoped for me and June and all of Ridge Creek that the answer was yes.

"You know, I think when Franklin first created those ripples he was just out joyriding on his mower. You know, for the pure love of grass and turf," Marcus said. "It was the rest of us that pictured our place for skipping rocks right here in the field."

It was funny, the way Marcus was all of a sudden such an expert in something so important to baseball when he didn't even want to play it. And that's when I realized.

"That's why you're the Skipper, Marcus," I said. "That's why Franklin named you that."

"Why's that?"

"You know that's what they call the manager of a ball club, right?"

Marcus looked at me like I'd asked him to plant daisies in the outfield.

"Seriously, Marcus? You really have been ignoring everything Lump's been teaching you about baseball

all these years, haven't you? No wonder he dropped his glove in left field and bolted that day."

"The skipper is the manager?" Marcus's voice was so small I had to stare at his lips to understand for sure what he said.

"He's the leader, the strategy-thinker-upper, the boss man. In charge of all this . . ." I waved my arm toward the rest of the broken and beautiful stadium. "That's you."

Marcus's face crumpled into a look that mixed sheer happiness with needing to throw up, and I let him have a minute. This time it wasn't because I was one of those friends who understood the quiet, but because something had caught my eye as I swept my palm out toward home.

The Rockskippers hadn't shown up for work yet, and if Ferdie was around, he was doing a pretty good job of ignoring us. I had thought Marcus and I were the only ones there. But high above the field in the bleachers, in the closest thing we had to the nose-bleeds and right where the sun set every night, sat . . . somebody.

Marcus mumbled something about the Skipper and the ripples and if I didn't mind could we just meet up later after he finished his very important job. I didn't pay him much attention or answer him or even take that handful of grass for Peter. I was too busy trying to figure out what Garland, who never, ever entered the stadium, was doing up there.

Sixteen

THERE wasn't any more time to wonder about Garland, because I had to see about Triple. I ran and I ran and I pulled in air and pushed it out and tried to ignore how breathing felt like swallowing a sack of knives.

The sweet honeysuckle gate let me through, and a clap of thunder shattered the sky right when I reached the other side. The rain didn't stretch to there — the treetops were the only thing above, and they kept things nice and safe and still.

Except then there was Triple, all alone on the banks of the creek and at the other end of my broken promise. He kneeled over Peter, who was about as still as the rock he was sitting on. I tried to calm my nerves and my brain and not scare either one of them by getting too close too quick, but Triple must have heard me.

"We're busy." He didn't look up.

And then that storm did roll in, through my words and out my soul. "Triple, that dumb turtle is slow as molasses 'cause he's supposed to be, and a championship day for a turtle involves swimming, sunbathing, and probably a good handful of worms." I threw a rock as hard as I could, right into the shallow part so it splashed all of us — Triple and Peter and me. Even Twang was there, balanced on a rock, just waiting for his turn again.

I don't think even Betsy Plogger would have done that. It wasn't a real good way to say sorry.

Triple stared at me and I stared right back. If his arms had been any longer than seven years, I bet he would have pushed me in. Instead, he did something worse. He ignored me. He looked down at Peter and got back to business like I wasn't even there.

"Triple —" I hoped he could hear the tone in my voice that said *I am here* and *I am sorry* and *I love you very much.*

But nothing.

"Look, I'm so sorry. I should have been here earlier, 'cause I said I would be. And I'm just —"

"Yeah, *sorry*," he said. "You said that already."

It had taken a whole bunch of years for choppy

water to create the curves on those rocks we stood on, but it took only a morning to dig a deep rut between the two of us.

And then, because June had done it to me first, I thought the mama thing to do would be to hug him, to squeeze him good whether he wanted it or not. Peter and Twang were between me and the rock closest to Triple, but with Garland's Grill and living on a moving vehicle, navigating tricky spaces was usually something I did real good.

Triple still wouldn't look at me, so I took the biggest leap I could without a running start. And I misjudged the length of my legs by about a summer or two, so rather than landing on the rock with my feet, I landed on it with my face.

My chin smacked it, and for a split second I saw sunglasses and stars and pies and birds, but once those birds fluttered away and the pain moved in, I was wet and cold and hurting. But Triple, he was there. He stuck out his skinny arm and dragged me from the shallow water to the slippery shore.

"I'm sorry. I'm sorry." I was somewhere between whispering and wailing, and somehow the rain had pierced through the trees and poured on everything, not caring what it touched.

"Derby, you're bleeding!" Triple yelled.

What I'd thought was rain wasn't, and my sleeve streaked red after I ran it across my chin. I opened and closed my jaw to be sure it was still screwed on tight, which made Triple gasp like it would crack clean off.

"I'm all right. It's okay, Triple." I pulled him down next to me. He stuck Peter in his lap, Peter, who seemed to like the pitter-patter of the rain.

Grit and sand burned inside the cut the creek had given me. The muddy water was all I had to wash it out with, but Garland had taught me about getting things done. So I did, and we were quiet for a bit.

"Peter's a good turtle," I said after a while, and when I did, he crawled from Triple's lap to mine.

"Even if he's not, Charlie still hasn't shown her face down here yet. She might be all out of practice," said Triple.

"Or turtles," I said. Triple laughed a little at that but not all the way, so I could tell he wasn't finished with being mad. "Marcus can help us feed him real good too," I continued. "We won't tell Charlie that the best turtles have this newfangled *vegetaaaarian* diet."

And so we sat there on a wet rock underneath a wetter rain. And when our conversation and the rain dried up, we figured it was time to go back to the Rambler and maybe do the onions.

Triple stood up with Peter in his hands. "Do you have Twang?"

"Don't *you* have Twang?" I asked.

I'd been too worried about a broken promise and a scraped-up chin, overgrown weeds and Garland in the nosebleeds. All of those things had blinded me from keeping safe the very thing that Triple loved most.

I think we both saw it at the same time — down where the creek opened up into the river, past where Garland said we were allowed to wade. Twang's paper-towel tube bobbed in and under the creek's current, mad like the storm. I must have kicked Twang when my feet flew out from under me. Anyone else would have thought it was garbage, but Triple and I watched his heart and soul and what used to be our mama's sandals float away right downstream.

"You wrecked everything," Triple said, so quiet it sounded like the wind blew his words.

And then he tucked Peter under his arm and walked away, up to the honeysuckle and Queen Anne's lace, alone.

Seventeen

AT the Rambler, where Garland was closer to the earth, he was back to his jolly old self. The only problem was that he saw my face before I could ask him about being in the nosebleeds.

"Are the turtles fighting back now?"

Garland was like a magnet, and with that teasing nudge, I snapped right into him.

"What'd you do to this girl, Triple?" he asked over my shoulder, which bristled me all up, afraid Triple would tell the truth. I didn't need eyes in the back of my head to see Triple stiffen up too. But he didn't say anything.

"I'm fine, Garland. Just misjudged the rocks down at the creek. A clumsy girl in wide open spaces, you know."

Garland paused like he didn't really buy it. But he didn't ask, and I didn't tell him. And before I knew it, he was washing the sting off my chin and finding me an icepack like any good mama would.

"Well, you can't tell it by these clothes, but it looks like the rain's about over," Garland said. "You two heading over to the stadium?"

That's when someone knocked on the Rambler's door. Garland swung it in fast, probably surprised that we had a visitor here. The Grill was where we welcomed the town — he doesn't even hang a Christmas wreath on the door of the Rambler, because it's mostly for closing up his sadness while the hope stays on the outside.

"Well, look who it is!" Garland's hello was so loud that I jumped a little. Or maybe also because of who was on the other side.

Betsy Plogger's who it was, that's why.

"Hey," she said. "Aunt Candy wanted you to have this." She handed Garland a Famous Apple, just like the one I'd left on June's porch, hidden from the rain. It was hard to see under her umbrella, but I was pretty sure she was trying not to look around too much in the Rambler as some odd show of respect or something. My stomach flipped a little at seeing those soft edges to her, even though it was silly that she was still protecting her hairdo when it was hardly raining.

"Thank you, Miss Plogger!" said Garland.

Nobody said anything for a minute. Garland had one arm on the door and one under the pie, and both of us were looking at this unusual visitor like she was a baby squirrel that had dropped right out of a nest and onto our stoop.

"Are you all right?" Betsy tipped the edge of the umbrella up enough for me to see that she meant it.

"Oh," I said. "I fell in the creek."

"Okay." Betsy took one step backwards, and then almost smiled at me.

"Okay," I said.

"She'll have more pies at the Rally, of course, but I think she's been practicing so she can beat those chocolate chip cookies."

"Sounds familiar," Garland said, looking back to Triple.

And when Garland spun around in search of a fork, I watched Betsy curl around the Rambler, back to the Heritage Inn. But I couldn't linger too long on whatever had just happened, because it was time to get to the game. Garland would have to do the prep on his own.

"Triple," I said, "you ready?"

"No way," he said, eyes only for Peter. Triple wasn't at all interested in the game. A flicker of Twang washing down the creek made me remember why real quick.

"Come on. I know where we can get him some really good grass clippings," I said. "Let me just get on some clothes that weren't in the creek and we can get there early for batting practice."

But when I came back from the queen room, Christmas Nutmeg and all, Triple was gone.

"Pie?" Garland hadn't even bothered with a plate. But I just left, and I didn't even say *Goodbye* or *No, thank you* or *What were you doing in the nosebleeds?*

It's funny how you can be lonely even with people on all sides of you — I had a sea of them from here to the outfield. Triple was who knows where, sulking about Twang and as mad as a dove in a mud puddle. Marcus was in the bullpen and June was probably with him, and Garland sure wouldn't be in the stands again, not twice in one day.

So there I was as soon as the game began, all

alone behind the dugout with a busted-up chin. The thing about baseball is that it moves real slow and gives you enough time to sit with yourself and your thoughts, and so that's what I did. But the other thing about baseball is that it's easy to get caught up in the ceremony of it, and when the third-base side starts the wave, you stand up and sit down with the whole crowd, alone or not. After a couple loops of that wave, it started to fizzle out — people returned to their hot dogs and claps, trying to keep up with whatever tune Miss Houston was working out.

Except then I heard something small and shrieking, something that wasn't letting the wave crash, and it was coming from way over by third base.

"One!" someone screeched.

"Two!" another yelled.

Betsy and Lollie both screamed, "Three!" at the very same time.

It took another couple rounds of those girls' directions, but the wave started up again, and when it was good and going, going, gone, it made it all the way to Marcus and June in the bullpen. Betsy and Lollie jumped up and down and hugged each other, and even the other team's left fielder gave them a little nod.

The stadium's energy made me forget a little bit about my face and my loneliness. But then the middle of the fifth inning rolled around, and Marcus rolled out of the bullpen. June stood watch right inside, her hand on her heart. She looked like she wanted to ride along with him, just for the spin of it, just to be with the Skipper, one of her memories on the outside.

And then I had a thought.

Marcus.

Who knew a lot about turf management.

Maybe I could fix something after all.

While he finished grooming the red dirt and headed back toward the bullpen, a big voice came over the loudspeaker. *"Ladies and gentlemen! Are you hungry for Estelle Hooch's chocolate chip cookies? Maybe Candy Plogger's famous apple pie? Want to dunk your favorite Rockskipper or try to steal their bases? Race a turtle? Throw a knuckleball? The Rally for the Rockskippers, Ridge Creek's favorite night of the summer, is coming up on the longest day of the year. More daylight means more fun! Tickets available at the box office!"*

The Rally was a big day for June. She had the regular game tickets to deal with, and then the dunk tickets and softball registrations and tickets for pie-tasting too.

She'd be here, and we could be there.

It would be the perfect day for a housewarming and a homecoming.

JUNE 12

Eighteen

SUMMER began to peel back its layers, and the next few days were a blur of Rockskippers and Rally hopes. Triple hadn't talked to me since that day at the creek, and I hadn't had a minute to catch up with Marcus on account of his turf management. I'd had to wait for the first Rockskippers' road trip, when he wouldn't be so busy. The Grill wasn't as crowded when the team was traveling, but you could always count on the regulars. And since I knew our best customer would be having extra mustard, I made sure to fill those tubs up.

When you fill up the mustard tubs, though, you aren't supposed to drop the biggest one on the ground. And if you've never seen how far mustard can splatter when it belly-flops on the pavement — well, it's farther than you think. Your fingernails will be yellow for days, no matter how many times you scrub them in the creek or the sink.

I just stared at the mess, one more thing to fix.

But since Marcus was one of those friends who can read the different kinds of quiets, when he stumbled upon me and the mustard, he got the rags from Garland.

"At least it wasn't ketchup, or we'd have a crime scene on our hands." Marcus scraped yellow from the concrete canvas.

"At least red's a Rockskipper color," I said. "Can you meet at the marquee tonight? I've got an idea."

"I'll bring a new penny," Marcus said, and that was that.

Triple was in the Grill with Garland, and their operation was in full force without any room for me. "We're good on the mustard," I yelled up to them.

If they had looked at me, they would have had a thousand jokes about how the mustard was good on me instead. But neither one had any jokes to tell. Triple was still silent, and Garland was only acting merry to the masses on the outside, as though Triple had told him how much I'd ruined. I went in anyway, even though there wasn't room for all of us, because I wasn't sure where else to be.

And that's how we spent the next hour—the nuts and bolts of an assembly line humming along and all greased up. But really, each part was rusted.

After the last burger had been flipped and the oil stopped bubbling, Triple threw his apron onto the floor and left. I think he meant to hit the hook behind the door and couldn't see through his madness, so I hung it where it belonged.

Garland scrubbed the counter with his back to me, but must have felt me trying to come up with something to say. So he did instead. "Go talk to him, Derby."

"Okay," I said, and headed back to the Rambler.

Triple was lying on his back on the top bunk, nose almost to the ceiling. I couldn't see his eyes, but I could tell he was crying. My heart dared me to break the silence before Garland came back. But Triple did first.

After a long pause and a few snuffles, I heard a quiet "I miss that shoebox."

"I know. It was an accident. I didn't mean to—I'm sure you had Twang all safe and sound until my grand nosedive." I sat down on the bunk underneath and thought about our mama's sandals, and how she'd hardly ever seen Triple walking around in his own shoes.

My eyes were squished shut so tight that I didn't see Triple's feet swing down from the top bunk. But the next thing I knew, Triple was sitting next to me. He wrapped one skinny arm around my shoulder, his other hand on my knee. That dirty little hand said *I've got you now* and *It'll all be fine* and *I love you too*.

"Thanks, Triple." I had to answer with real words.

"Might've been me who kicked Twang off that rock. I forgot about him for a while 'cause of Peter. Maybe he felt mad about that." Triple was so tender-hearted toward the things he loved.

"Maybe. But I bet you felt mad at me 'cause I forgot about you for a while too. So that makes sense."

"Yeah."

"You know Miss June? She's needed some help." I grabbed Triple's little hand. "And I have too, and so we've been fixing up each other's broken parts, even though she doesn't all the way know it yet."

"She probably misses her groundskeeper, right, Derby?" Triple's sincere truth made me smile a little. The impatiens had revealed that tidbit.

"Yeah, she does—and someone else, too. Kinda like us. We miss someone, but Garland is still here, and aren't we lucky to have him? But June is all out of someones."

"Oh." Triple said a lot in that syllable. "She needs a new song, too."

I nodded, and just as our meeting on the mound was coming to a sweet close, the door to the Rambler swung open and Garland came home.

Nineteen

IT had taken a lot of grease splatters to get to that point with Triple, and it looked like this summer would be one for blisters, too. Because that's what it would take for my plan. So that night I headed out to the marquee, out to Marcus.

It was one of those nights that didn't get all the way dark, like maybe the sun wasn't quite done shining for the day. And in that almost-haze, I could see the marquee shouting **ON SATURDAYS, TAKE THEM OUT TO THE BALL GAME! KIDS UNDER 6 FREE!**, which was maybe how old I was when I'd met Marcus.

"Hey," he said.

"Hey," I said right back. "What do you think about Betsy Plogger?"

"Betsy? I mean, I try not to think of her so much at all." Marcus wiped sweat from his face and left a trail of bullpen dust behind.

"But she's not all that bad, right?"

"I guess," said Marcus. "She brought me a pie."

"She did? Candy's Famous Apple?"

Marcus rubbed his belly like the thought of it was pouring actual sugar right back in there, crystal by lump by cube. "No," he said. "It was the chocolate chiffon."

It sank in slow what Betsy might have meant by the chocolate chiffon, but if she had a crush on Marcus Emmett, I did not want to be the one to spill the beans. I couldn't tell how much room he had under his shaggy curls, but his head didn't need to get much bigger than it was. Maybe that's why she'd smiled at me earlier. Or maybe she was a little like me, not real sure where she belonged.

"Hmm," I said. "I guess pies are vegetarian, right?"

"I don't know about that, but I do know they are delicious."

That's when Ferdie walked by, carrying a broom in one hand and his box of letters in the other. He walked over real slow, and since he doesn't say much, I thought his eyes were about to make us leave.

"Evening," he said, easy and gentle and more welcoming than I expected. I think I said hello.

"Ferdie," Marcus said, and shook his hand like a grownup would.

"I found this while I was sweeping up inside. Will it work?" Ferdie handed something to Marcus, something too small for me to see. But I knew. Whatever year it was, I bet Marcus agreed that it was nice to be remembered.

"All right," Ferdie said, tipping his cap to us and letting us be. He shuffled away about as slow as he'd shown up, like maybe by making his rounds at a speed like molasses, he wouldn't have to go to wherever his home was. We all had overlapping strands of that, and I wondered how his story wove into this stadium that wrapped us all up in it.

That's when Marcus flashed me the penny, shiny and new and stamped with this year.

"Ferdie!" I yelled at his back. "Do you like sweet-potato fries?"

He turned real slow, the way an owl watches the night. "Yes, ma'am," he said.

"Okay, then. Come by sometime."

After Ferdie shuffled off again, it was just me and Marcus, watching the last grip the sun had on the day, sitting there until the true night moved in.

"That first marquee was his idea." Marcus looked up. "The one about Franklin."

"He told you?" I asked. "He doesn't say much, does he?"

"He sticks to what matters," Marcus said. "Things like Franklin and June."

"Franklin and June," I echoed.

It was time to get Marcus in on my plan. So I asked him, and then I folded my Christmas Nutmeg smile into two straight lines of wait and hope and see.

"That's a real busy day. I won't have much time," Marcus said. "And won't she be working?"

"Exactly," I said. "That's why it's best."

Marcus didn't ask me anything else — he knew, he trusted, he nodded.

And then we pressed that penny between our thumbs and wished real good. I don't know how wishes work, or if you wreck them by wishing for more than one thing at a time, but that's what I did. A wish had already worked with Triple, even without the penny, so it was worth trying for a bunch more.

I wished for the Skipper to patch up a garden.

I wished for something sweet of my own from Betsy.

I wished I knew why Garland had snuck up to the nosebleeds.

I wished June would tell me about her daughter.

I wished the sun could stay out longer and longer and that this summer wouldn't ever end.

JUNE 13

Twenty

IT was a good morning for strawberries.

I walked up and down the numbered aisles of the Sweet Street Mart, holding my nose on the odds because a girl can only take all that pickle smell about half the time. This place was a mishmash of stuff: worms (both for bait and the gummy kind), newspapers from the city that probably only got bought for the crossword, and cherry colas where they squirt sugary syrup right into the fizz. They've got apples and bananas and laundry detergent, and they've got the Ploggers every single morning.

"Morning." Because I was on aisle seven, I said that with my nose shut tight, so even though I thought I was being polite and friendly, I might not have looked it.

"Hey, Derby," Betsy said, her voice some kind of suspicious.

Thank goodness she followed me over to aisle eight.

"Are you looking forward to the Rally?" I asked her, nose un-pinched.

The last few years Betsy and Lollie had begged Goose and Scooter to let them turn just one parking spot into a beauty parlor, and they'd given pedicures and manicures to anyone who would let them. Once, Lump Emmett had them paint his toenails with some gold sparkles for good luck, and they charged him extra 'cause his feet were so big. Marcus was horrified, but Lump did run a little extra fast at the game that night.

"Yeah," she said. "Are you?"

"No better way to spend the longest day of the year, right?"

But the thing was, I had other plans for that long day, and there wouldn't be much room for painting nails.

Betsy and I walked, maybe even together, to the produce aisle. She ripped a bag off the spinner and picked over the apples — a green, a red, some pinks, dropping them all down into the bag.

"For Aunt Candy," she said. "She likes a bunch of all of them, but I prefer the pinks, so."

I wasn't real sure what to say to her, so I got busy figuring out which of the strawberries June and I might prefer, even though there's not a bad strawberry in the summertime.

"Plus they're vegetarian," I said after we'd picked out our apples and strawberries, and I meant it.

Betsy looked at me, and then she took her big bag of apples up to the cash register and off she went. That's when I wondered if maybe June liked apples too, and I plucked out a few good pinks.

I took my strawberries and apples and walked back up the street to the stadium, where it was still too early for the baseball players. My real favorite players were already hard at work — Marcus in the bullpen and June settling into her box office, ready to welcome the crowd. Maybe even Ferdie, fixing up the marquee.

"Knock, knock," I said, and spun past the pennants.

"My girl," June said. "There she is."

It made my stomach bubble up like the onion-ring

oil when she said that, both because I was so happy to be her girl and also because I wondered about her other girl, who seemed to be nowhere close.

"You're looking a little better," June said when she saw my face.

"Wouldn't be summer without a bunch of Band-Aids," I said.

"Well," June said, "doesn't change your smile."

"I brought you some strawberries and apples," I said. "Betsy had a real good idea about some pinks, and so here we go."

June and I sat on the stadium's front steps, right back onto those Rockskipper seat cushions, swatting the flies that tried to taste the fruit.

"Betsy?"

"I know." I took a big, loud bite of an apple to get busy with something else.

"Lump Emmett says she's real good at pedicures," June said. "My hands might be past nail-painting age, but maybe she can fix me up at the Rally." I got stuck somewhere between thinking that was a spectacular idea and not liking it at all, not liking the sharing-June-with-Betsy-Plogger part.

June inspected her wrinkly, rough hands, and

then pressed them to her face. "They're not what they used to be."

"How long have you known Ferdie?" I asked her, trying to change the subject from something small that I didn't like to something big that she might not want to remember. They must have shared Franklin if they had shared tissues.

Instead of moving her hands away, June scrunched them higher up toward her temples, rubbing them in a way that said it was a long story to tell. But she started anyway.

"Ferdie? He's been a friend to our family since the early days. Used to play ball right on this field before it had all these metal seats wrapped around it. That's how once-upon-a-time works, did you know?"

I didn't.

"It's what you know all about, things changing and the times along with it. Once-upon-a-time becomes the *next thing* upon a time."

My mama was the once-upon-a-time, and June was the next thing.

"What was here once upon a time?"

"An empty lot — a bunch of dirt and boys and ball. A bunch of friends."

I wanted to ask about her once-upon-a-time girl, and what happened next, but I'd almost finished up the strawberries and June's not-painted fingernails were still up near her head.

"Took a while for this place to grow on Ferdie, but he'll be here caring for it as long as it takes."

Above, Ferdie's marquee said **POSTER NIGHT! KEEP THE ROCKSKIPPERS AT HOME EVEN WHEN THEY'RE AWAY!**

"Well, he told me he liked sweet-potato fries, so maybe next time you come by the Grill, you can bring him along? He's never come before."

"Yes, ma'am," June said, and we ate the rest of the strawberries.

Twenty-One

SMEARED on some Christmas Nutmeg before I walked into the Heritage Inn to use the facilities. Lollie Plogger was right there in the lobby.

"Derby!" she said, looking left and right and left again — maybe watching for Betsy, maybe since she sounded happy to see me and shouldn't have.

"Hey, Lollie," I said. "What are you doing?"

"Well, Betsy decided to throw a fit about something, and my mom is up there trying to get her over it so she'll come with us to the drugstore. It was her idea, to get supplies for the Rally."

"Interesting," I said, and it was.

"I mean, you know Betsy," Lollie said, and shook her head the way Garland did when someone told him they didn't believe in Santa Claus.

Without Betsy nearby, it was almost like Lollie was in charge now, standing there like she'd been trying on her mama's confidence. It looked good on her, even if she had to grow into it a little. Since my mind hadn't been all the way changed on Betsy Plogger, that thought made me crinkle my nose so I wouldn't let out a laugh.

"Bless you," Lollie said.

"Lollie, what? Bless me?" The laugh slipped out and felt real good.

"Yeah. Uncle Scooter taught me that. If you think you're gonna sneeze and someone says *Bless you*, you don't. And if you are all alone and nobody can bless you, you just think *Blue cow* over and over and over again until you're not making that funny face anymore."

"Well, I'll have to remember that. Sometimes we kick up a lot of pepper in Garland's Grill," I said. "Good luck with Betsy." And I thought I mostly meant it.

It was hot outside, the kind of hot that made the creek feel extra nice, and that's when I remembered Triple down there, all alone with Peter. I still owed him a lesson in Rockskipper high-fives, with or without Twang.

Marcus and I met up in the parking lot, him on the tail end of his groundskeeper lunch break and me free from getting blessed by Lollie Plogger. We didn't have a lot of time, but I had to show him how I thought our plan would work.

"Marcus," I said, "we've got to go through the stadium to get there."

"What if June sees us? And besides, if Ferdie sees me now, then I'm going to have to get back to work. He's an honest kind of guy, and the Skipper is too." Marcus reminded me a little of Lollie just then, with how he puffed up his chest and acted bigger than his britches.

"Lunch break, Marcus," I said. "You still have some time. It's a Rally emergency anyway, and that's a high priority for the turf-management team, right?"

He couldn't say anything to that, even though I was exaggerating a bunch. So the two of us scraped our shins through the wide row of grass and gravel that separated the Heritage Inn's parking lot from the back side of the James Edward Allen Gibbs Stadium. Marcus ran his fingers along the boards, knowing just where to hop them up to avoid the splinters, and then the two of us slipped right between the bowing boards.

"Grass, Marcus," I said. "For Peter."

Marcus looked at me real funny, but he still made

a beeline for the bullpen, and I followed close behind. I only peeked up once to see if Garland was in the nosebleeds, and when I saw that he wasn't, I bumped right into the back end of Marcus.

"Derby, honestly," he said. "We're about to go see June's house and you said it was full of weeds, right? Is Peter too good for that kind of green?"

He wasn't, of course. He was just a turtle. But there was some kind of magic in the stadium's grass, and that's what Triple deserved.

Marcus picked up a white plastic bag that used to have pistachios in it and maybe even still had some spit-out shells, and that's what he used to stuff some grass clippings in.

It would have to do.

"Come on," he said, and we ran through the outfield, past where Lump had left him alone on Thanksgiving Day.

Marcus hopped up into the corner seats where left field became the infield, right at the edge of the away team's dugout. He snaked up through a few rows, and I was right behind him, the Skipper. We were two ghosts of the season, slipping through time and traditions only to slide out again. And then we were outside once more and it was my turn to lead.

It took as long to get to the Mattingly house as it did to get an order at Garland's Grill on a day that the Rockskippers lose, when everyone wants ice cream. Scooping takes a lot of muscle that Triple doesn't have yet, so you'd better not be in a rush. It wasn't that June's house was too far away, but Marcus and I slowed down. I think we were both a little nervous about this plan's bigness.

Once we got there, I saw again how bad it was.

"I don't know too much about flowers," Marcus said.

"Yeah, but how hard could it be to rip these out and plant some new ones?"

We crouched down by the bed under the mailbox's sun that always shone, not sure whether to pull a flowering weed or leave it. And that was only the beginning. We stayed slow and hushed while we wandered around, because this place deserved some kind of reverence. I'd have to figure out what to do with the frog-sized gulp in my throat in order to say anything anyway.

"It's everywhere," Marcus said, pushing piles of

this and that out of the way with his feet so he'd have a place to step.

I armed myself with sticks and twigs and flowers that had wilted right off a magnolia tree, and said, "I know."

"Even this door could use some sprucing up, don't you think, Derby?"

And he was right. The paint on the front door was chipped, a faded red like the one at the stadium, and even though that had probably been happening before Franklin died, it looked extra sad peeking out over the yard like that.

"I wonder if Garland has a wreath to share," I said, blowing off the spiderwebs as best I could. "She might not want to remember Christmas all the time like he does, though."

I whispered that last part a little, but it felt real loud in my gut. Marcus took a handful of sticks out of my grip and we stood there on the porch like we'd just knocked and were waiting to be invited in.

"We can do this," I said, or breathed or felt or something.

"Rally caps, for sure," said Marcus.

Twenty-Two

WHEN we got back within spitting distance of the stadium, Marcus retraced our steps to get back to work and I swiped on some Christmas Nutmeg to undo the sweat and add some kind of glamour. Sneaky like the stadium pigeons, I rounded the corner out front to get closer to the box office, closer to the pennants, closer to June.

"Derby?"

A small voice came from the steps. It belonged to Betsy, and there she was, right under the marquee. Before, I would have thought she was sitting alone because she'd bossed everyone right out of the picture, but now she was a snapshot of lonely.

"Betsy, hi," I said, gentle like you would be if you saw a broken-winged bird. "What are you doing here?"

She sighed a dramatic *Woe is me* kind of sigh, but

I believed her. "Lollie and I were supposed to be planning the Rally booth. We're the best at painting nails, you know."

"I know," I said.

"Aunt Candy said she'd take us to the drugstore to stock up, and I said it didn't even matter to me what the colors were, as long as they were beautiful and not tested on animals."

"Right. Vegetarian."

"And then Aunt Candy laughed at me but Lollie didn't say anything and so they went without me because I wouldn't come out of the bathroom and I really hope they got the best pinks." Betsy unraveled right before my eyes.

I didn't really know what to say, mostly because I'd seen the other half of this ruckus in the lobby at the Heritage Inn. Plus, Triple and Garland and I had never had a conversation about nail polish, so I didn't have any *Been there, done that* wisdom for her.

"I wouldn't come out because I cut my hair," Betsy said, and she really had.

She shook out a sloppy ponytail to show me what was left over. Her bathroom floor must have looked like the bullpen with all its grass clippings strewn about in clumps and piles — that's how much she'd hacked off.

"Oh." It was all I could find.

Miss Houston's organ was warming up behind us, providing a soundtrack for this moment that was equal parts horror and sympathy.

"Well, don't you both look like somebody trampled through your rosebuds?" That was June, and Betsy and I looked up at her in sync. "I can fix this. Come on." June probably meant Betsy's unfortunate haircut, but the way she said it made me think that she could have fixed the impatiens and the Christmas wreath and the peeling paint too. But the storm that had trampled through *her* rosebuds was too much, too strong, too gray.

And so, believe it or not, we went to her house, the three of us.

June ushered us in with all the tenderness and care she would use for picking up shattered glass. There I was again, inside the front hall with an invitation this time, a moving picture by the wall of stills. And then I caught a whiff of something sweet, a fresh smell, one that traveled farther than the mustiness that clung to the walls.

"Strawberries." June answered the question I hadn't even asked yet.

"Smells delicious," Betsy said, and I agreed.

While June went ahead of us, we stayed back. It was hot, so maybe it was the sight of the girl that made my skin go goosebumps.

The pictures on the wall showed a family of three at birthdays and barbecues and celebrating the first day of school. June and Franklin were so young once, and even though they got older as the wall got longer, they were always looking at the girl. All three of them were dancing, dancing all the way down the hall. The scenes spoke of that girl's shyness and her spunk. In just a few steps she grew up from a little thing to a girl my age, riding a lawn mower. And then there she was, nearly grown, in right field at the James Edward Allen Gibbs Stadium, wearing jean shorts, saddle shoes, and a grounds-crew cap.

"Wow," I said, and this time it was Betsy who agreed.

I didn't hear June slip behind us until she clanked some ice against the sides of a glass. Maybe it was to get our attention, or maybe she was as startled as I was by that photograph.

"Franklin took that one. That's why she's laughing so hard. He was too, which is why it's a little blurry. Stole her daddy's heart more often than she stole his riding lawn mower." June handed us each a glass of lemonade, and used the cool napkin left over to dampen her sweaty forehead.

"Who is she?" I barely heard myself ask.

"That's our girl, our one and only." I heard a smile in June's voice, even though the sparkle in her eye was turning a bit watery. "That's Phoebe Susan."

Of course June had to go and have a daughter with the most beautiful name I had ever heard. I'd thought the name June was glamorous, but *Phoebe Susan* was exquisite.

"She's pretty." Betsy nudged me a little, reminding me to snap out of it or say something, and that's when I realized who she was.

Sugar Sue.

Twenty-Three

WHAT happened to her?" I whispered it.

June smoothed the wrinkles in her dress, wrinkles that were a little bit darker because some sweat had soaked through. "Come into the kitchen, girls. Let's have a bite. It's late for lunch."

Betsy and I followed her into the kitchen, where a wide-open window was covered with a thin curtain that didn't budge because there wasn't any breeze to make it dance. A small fan on the counter tried to help, but it didn't look like it had many nods left in its neck. June turned a little toward us and a little toward the counter, where she sliced cucumbers and tomatoes and slathered mayonnaise on pieces of white bread. The sweat was shiny on her face, not at all dusty like the pictures on the wall.

And then she smiled a sad kind of smile. One like the Rockskippers had the other night during the fifth inning, the kind that turns mostly down and barely up.

"We lost her right when she'd barely finished being a teenager. It was an accident at the creek, and she slipped under its current and drifted away." June stopped talking for a moment, but she didn't lose the look on her face.

"The creek," I said, looking for some kind of answer in my own wrinkled napkin.

I thought about my creek, where Triple lost his best thing and was probably alone right then and where Garland didn't let us go out too far. The creek, where Marcus had taught me all the best Rockskipper high-fives. The creek, where Betsy never showed up thanks to her hairdos and pedicures. It was strange to think of June and Franklin and me and Marcus knowing the same place so well, sharing some mysterious roots.

That sad tale must have been a hard secret to keep. And I couldn't figure out why June had decided to tell it now, just to me and Betsy Plogger.

Betsy picked up a folded-over newspaper and used it as a fan. When she noticed me looking, she pulled out the sports page and gave it to me.

"Thanks," I whispered to her, and she smiled back.

"You've always reminded me of her, Derby," June said. "You have her curiosity and the same disheveled head of hair hiding a brain so smart, the same ragged T-shirts that can't contain a heart of love and good. You've got the same smile that can light up a stadium."

"Thank you, June." I still could only whisper.

"You're welcome, Sugar Sue."

June brought over three plates of tomato-and-cucumber sandwiches and strawberries, a shaker of salt, and a bamboo fan that was a whole lot fancier than the sports page. "Show me something, Betsy," she said. "I bet you've got a smile underneath there too." She grabbed a hand of each of us from across the table. I should have been mad that I was somehow sharing this moment with Betsy Plogger, but knowing she had the same mama-sized hole as me had changed my mind on her.

And then Betsy smiled.

We didn't talk about the heat as it rose or why a puddle of candle wax was stuck to the middle of the table, right in between our hands. June said she'd fix Betsy's hair, but I think we all needed more fixed than that.

So there at the kitchen table, Betsy told her story again. I helped out with some of the details this time, so June got the facts rather than the flair. And over three lemonades, three tomato-and-cucumber sandwiches, and a centerpiece of freshly picked Queen Anne's lace, Betsy made her second new friend of the summer.

"Stay here a minute." June disappeared from the table, taking her bamboo fan with her.

Betsy looked at me. "I know she belongs to you, Derby."

My heart sank like an anchor tied to all the bricks in the world. That's when I knew that it wasn't true. June didn't belong only to me. She belonged to all of Ridge Creek, even Betsy. But June and I had a foundation built on spending summers and the rest of the year with boys — the Rockskippers and Franklin, Garland and Triple. It was built on sharing Marcus, even before he was the Skipper. It was built on lemonades and lipstick and laughing on the front porch, and it was somehow built on the family we'd had once upon a time.

And now it was built on making room for Betsy.

"Found what I was looking for," said June, waltzing back to the table. She handed something small to Betsy, studying her face as their hands touched.

Betsy's expression matched what she read from the tube. "'Heavens to Betsy.'" June and I smiled at each other while she twisted it open and stared at how beautiful it was. And when June handed her a small pearl mirror, she smeared the lipstick on and gasped.

"The best pink," Betsy said.

The three of us finished our tomato-and-cucumber sandwiches and tried not to leave lipstick on the bread. Betsy forgot about her hair, but June didn't, and she trimmed it right up. I forgot about last summer's Betsy, and all of us forgot about the heat.

"We should get back to the stadium. Rally prep, right?" I didn't know if June meant her or us, but it didn't matter. She cleared our plates and put them in the sink, and while she puttered around the kitchen for another minute or two, Betsy and I snuck back to that wall of pictures.

"Look at this one, Derby—it's some kind of a wedding announcement in an old newspaper," Betsy said. "She was supposed to get married, June's daughter."

I'd missed it the last time I was there, when I'd broken in by accident. As soon as I read the printed words that were fading right back into the page, I swear that humid house gave me shivers.

ENGAGED TO BE WED:
MISS PHOEBE SUSAN MATTINGLY TO
MR. FERDINAND HENRY GLASGOW.
MR. AND MRS. FRANKLIN MATTINGLY
ARE PLEASED TO WELCOME HIM AS
THEIR SON FOREVER.

No wonder he'd been sharing tissues at Franklin's service. Ferdie was supposed to be June's real kind of family.

Twenty-Four

IT was hard to rally up any excitement for the afternoon's game, because my heart had already taken as much as I thought it could in one day. But then I saw Garland back at the Grill, and he was always good at making hope float on top again.

"Sunshine!" he said.

"Hey, Garland. Where's Triple?"

"You beat him this time," Garland said. "Peter made him forget all about the onions."

I took the pistachio-shell bag out of my pocket, the one that had Peter's deluxe meal inside, and set it on Garland's prep area, trying to be casual and not revealing the heartbeat that wanted to jump out of my skin.

"Do you know who Phoebe Susan is?" I asked.

"Is that Miss Houston's name?" Garland tied and retied his apron strings, and that's when I knew how deep June's once-upon-a-time was. Even Garland didn't know.

And then my shine turned back on a little, and I danced around the Grill doing the onions and prepping the mustard. When Triple hopped into the Grill, all three of us twirled around each other until Garland said that we both better get out of there because "Three's a lot of love, but three's also a crowd."

So I grabbed Peter's dinner and Triple's hand, and we headed out to the game.

"Here," I said, handing Triple the bag. "This is for Peter, the perfect vegetarian meal for a turtle."

"Pistachios?"

"Look inside," I said. "It's Rockskipper grass, straight from the outfield, so it's the most paid-attention-to lawn in all of Ridge Creek. And if you ever need any more, just go see Marcus in the bullpen. If you call him the Skipper, he'll do anything you want."

"Awesome," said Triple, and he stuck that dinner right in his pocket.

The sun beat down on the scene, on the line milling around June's box office and under Ferdie's words, which seemed so far from the words of Opening Day. The hot pavement seared through the soles of your sneakers if you stood in place for too long, so everyone had a little extra bounce in their step.

"How was the creek today?" I asked, afraid he'd bring up Twang, afraid he'd be upset that I'd missed another day for high-fives and turtle practice.

"Oh, Derby, it was awesome," Triple said. "Charlie came by looking for a new one today. She said she had to start over because her mom left the lid of the tank open and her best racer escaped."

"Well, that's a real shame," I said.

And I only sort of meant it. Triple had me and Garland as examples for how to treat people nice, and that was it. I didn't want him to grow up like a jerk, but I did want him to beat Charlie Bell.

"I know," he said. "Such a shame."

"Derby!" For the umpteenth time that day, my name spilled out of a Plogger's mouth, and mostly in a way that said *Hello* and *How are you* and *Nice to see you.*

"Hi, Lollie," I said, and thought an extra *Blue cow,* just in case a laugh might be coming on. "Betsy. You guys remember Triple, right?"

Triple seemed a little bit stunned by the two of them, because he turned the color of Heavens to Betsy itself. "Hey," he said, and ran up into the stadium.

"Do you want to sit with us tonight? We like the first-base side, and I know you guys are good bosses over there on the other," I said, not meaning bossy in a bad way, but it's what came out first.

"Sure," Lollie said. "Right, Betsy?"

"That'd be nice." She squeezed my hand on our way up to the seats, and as nice as Lollie was, it was even nicer to share a secret with only Betsy.

So the four of us got our Rockskippers posters and sat in the seats behind the first base dugout—Triple, Lollie, Betsy, and I. When Marcus caught my eye from the bullpen, he looked real confused. I just shrugged and laughed and was glad I could use the Heritage Inn bathroom for the rest of the summer without some kind of inquisition.

"Too bad Marcus won't be around, since he's so busy fixing up the grass," Betsy said when she saw me looking his way.

My loyalty to Marcus ran deeper than I could reach, because I blurted out, "Turf management, that's what it's called. It's not some old lady's gardening club."

Those Plogger ponytails whipped around in perfect precision, like they had planned a routine to start when someone said *turf management*. Triple looked at us like he'd rather be over there in the bullpen, and the three of us girls laughed, all together.

"It's so hot out here," Lollie said, after the laughing ran out. Betsy and I looked at each other, and I knew it was because this hot was nothing compared to the hot it had been in June's house. Where Marcus knew all about the outside, Betsy knew all about the inside.

"She needs a better fan, right?" I asked Betsy. "Or an air conditioner for her window or something?"

"She sure does. It's not right to be so lonely and miserable at the same time."

"Yeah," I said. "We can fix one of those parts, at least."

That's when Lollie grabbed Betsy's elbow to convince her it was time to start the wave, time to rally for the Rockskippers. So that's when I added a wrinkle to our plan to rally behind June. We could fix up the outside of her home, and we could cool down the inside. Ridge Creek was no place to be in the summer without air conditioning, especially if you lived in a real home that didn't have wheels and didn't have a fryer.

And then, as I stood up and sat down on the count of Betsy and Lollie's wave, watching Marcus rake the field free of bumps, I saw Ferdie across the way. Something in that moment stuck, and I wondered if I could make that something work.

I also wondered where I could find a bunch more pennies to wish on.

Twenty-Five

WHEN it was the top of the ninth inning and I was still thinking about those pennies, I figured it would be a good idea to leave early and get back to the Grill. The Rockskippers were up by a lot, so the bottom of the ninth wouldn't need to happen, and all of those fans would get a head start on their cheeseburgers and celebrating.

"Triple!" I yelled through my rolled-up poster, because my voice needed all the oomph it could get against the crowd. "Let's go!"

He was moving at the opposite speed of Peter, off collecting all kinds of things. From where I stood, it looked like leftovers and trash, but to Triple, it could have been an orchestra.

"Look," he said, walking over with a stack of popcorn buckets, so many that he had to use his chin to balance them. "This is awesome."

"I see that," I said. "Do you need some help?"

So Triple handed me a bunch of those buckets, and somehow I got the ones that still had kernels and crumbs inside.

"Do you think Peter would eat this?" I asked.

"Don't be ridiculous, Derby."

Blue cow.

"Okay, right," I said. "And what are your plans for these things?"

Triple looked at me with a face that was happier than I'd seen it all month, happier even than when he'd plucked Peter from the creek.

"Drums, Derby," he said. "The drums."

Blue cow. Blue cow. Blue cow.

"Well, okay. Let's go find you some drumsticks, kiddo," I said. Since he could still hardly see over his stack, I put my hand on his shoulder so he'd know when to turn and that I wasn't about to let *this* instrument face any danger.

We crossed back over to the spot we called home, stuck on that hot pavement like tar bubbles, squeezing everything we could out of this season. And when we got back to the Grill and Triple went to check on Peter, I took two of those popcorn buckets. He'd found so many, I didn't think he would even notice if a couple were gone. And even if he had, the Rock-skippers had a game the very next day and popcorn would be on the menu.

I grabbed the empty tip jar from the table outside where we kept the mustards. It wasn't so much a jar as a mustard tub that had run out a long time ago, but still, I snuck it back into my queen room with the popcorn buckets. And then I pulled the shower curtain door behind me and cut small rectangles out of my brand-new Rockskippers poster.

I taped a sign that said LUMP EMMETT to one popcorn bucket and FRANKLIN MATTINGLY to the other, and then I made a bigger sign that asked WHO'S YOUR FAVORITE ROCKSKIPPER? I loved Lump Emmett as much as anyone except for maybe Marcus and Mrs. Emmett. And I know Franklin wasn't ever on the team roster itself, but he sure was an honorary Rockshipper.

Between the two of them, I was sure we'd collect a whole bunch of extra tips tonight. If people had a choice, then taking just one of the buckets wasn't like I was stealing from the Grill. That's how I convinced myself that this wasn't a sneaky thing after all, even though I felt a little bit swoopy in my stomach.

So I stacked those two new tip buckets, stuck them under my arm, and grabbed two wooden spoons from the kitchenette so Triple would have a pair of drumsticks. Then I walked back over to the Grill like nothing important was happening.

"Derby," Garland said from above in the window, "can you help me out up here or what? That crowd storming over makes me think it was a winning kind of night."

I put the popcorn buckets down where the old tip jar used to be. My Christmas Nutmeg pocket had thirty-nine cents in it and the pennies were all old, so I threw that bunch of change into Franklin's bucket to get it started.

Twenty-Six

UNDER the marquee that night, Marcus and I counted the money from Franklin's bucket. He didn't let on whether he wondered about the one with his dad's name, colored in red marker and propped up by the mustards. And I didn't ask.

"How much do you think a fan costs? Or an air conditioner? They have those, right, for windows?" I didn't know too much about that, because the Rambler's air only worked if we were driving over sixty-five miles per hour, and Garland is, after all, a rambler.

Ridge Creek had given Franklin's bucket sixteen dollars and ninety-three cents' worth of wishes.

"Garland's letting you keep all these tips for June?" Marcus poked around in the bottom for the pennies. "But you'll need more than this for a fan."

It's funny how you think you are doing something nice for somebody else, and then something sweeps that feeling away, something that says Garland might not understand after all. He didn't know we'd had more tips than the ones I'd given him from the Lump bucket.

I didn't answer Marcus's question, just helped dig for shiny pennies. "Here's one," I said, grateful for its year.

I peeked at the marquee above, but this time it was empty. Ferdie had already taken the poster news down, making the stadium silent again. Marcus and I each put a thumb to that new penny, and I pushed a little extra hard because I thought that might help with the wishing.

"What did you wish for?" Marcus flicked the penny over his shoulder, and it spun around on its edge for a while before it settled down.

I didn't know if it was possible to feel something in common with a penny, but in those seconds while it tumbled, I knew exactly how it felt. The thing about wishes is that they are the same as secrets, only it's okay to keep them. But when Ferdie walked over with his box of letters, I wanted to spill my secrets and wishes and everything in between. I wanted all the wobbling to quit.

"This, this right here," I said. "This is what I wished for."

"The marquee?" Marcus asked. "I don't think it'll fit in the Rambler."

I gave Marcus a look that must have been one he'd seen before, because he said *Sorry* to me before I even squeaked out a syllable.

"I mean Ferdie. Here right now," I whispered, after accepting his apology and before Ferdie got close. Because our plan wasn't just about turf management and flowers.

"Evening," Ferdie said.

"Hi, Ferdie." I pulled Franklin's bucket onto my lap, trying to get out of his way and make him see me all at the same time. "You forgot to come by for sweet-potato fries!"

He laughed real slow and gravelly, like a wheelbarrow with a busted wheel that kept getting stuck on a rock. "One of these nights," he said, and that was good enough for me.

"Okay," I said. "And can we get into the stadium the night before the Rally? The right way?"

I thought by being honest about getting in on a non–game night, and not trying to sneak in through

FILLING and BELLIES, that I might be able to erase whatever that thing was, that thing I didn't want to admit, that thing that Garland might not understand after all.

But Marcus and Ferdie both looked at me like I'd asked to umpire the game itself.

"Please," I said. "It's for June."

Ferdie set his box of letters down and wiped some sweat from his lip with the collar of his shirt. And then he put his hands on his hips and said, "For her, anything."

I've believed in wishes ever since.

JUNE 20

Twenty-Seven

ON the eve of the Rally, the Ridge Creek Rock-skippers were probably all piled on a bus to-gether, making their way on back roads from a string of away games. They'd get the next morning to wash their uniforms and maybe eat breakfast with their families, and then it was time for their long day of getting honored and eating pie and exhausting them-selves before they had to get to work.

But before that happened, Marcus and I had some work of our own.

Since it was real late, everyone looked a little dif-ferent from how they did in the daytime. That must have been what the first day of school felt like when you hadn't seen a friend all summer, like the deep-down person you knew was there somewhere but it was a little hard to tell, with a new outfit and a sum-mer tan. Marcus had showered off all of the bullpen's grit, and it might have been the first time all summer that you could see the brown skin on his elbows. Betsy and Lollie came in matching pajamas — pink ones — because they'd told Candy that they weren't feeling too good, that it must have been something they'd eaten at the Grill, and that they were going to lie down in the lobby, where it was cooler.

I didn't have to worry about telling stories to get out of the Rambler, on account of my log-sawers back there. They'd sleep through anything.

Thanks to Ferdie, we got to walk in the front gate of the James Edward Allen Gibbs Stadium like proper guests. He carried a key ring that was as big around as a mixing bowl, and there were about twelve keys on it, jangling and clacking against each other like some fancy lady's jewelry.

He didn't say anything after he turned the key and swung open the gate. He only smiled the kind of smile you get when someone's unwrapping the birthday present you picked out for them, the smile that says, *I know this is what you wanted, and so it's become what I want too.*

I think he knows those boards in the outfield are still bent.

I think he likes sharing this place.

And then Ferdie handed me a different key, one that hung off a strap along with a whistle, and said, "In the dugout, next to the batting helmets."

"Thank you," I said, and the four of us ran into the dark stadium.

Marcus, Betsy, and Lollie followed me, and I snuck through the rip in the net behind home plate first.

"How did you know about this?" asked Betsy.

Marcus looked at her. "How did you not?"

"Marcus," I said, "that's not something the Skipper would say. Come on."

Betsy stuck her arm through the net, pink fingernails and all, and I reached out to help her squeeze through. I did the same for Lollie, but Marcus shook all six of our arms off. I think he feels more at home on a riding lawn mower than hanging out with girls in pink pajamas.

"You know we could have just hopped over the dugout from that front row," Marcus said. He was right, but some things are tradition.

I led the way to the dugout, Marcus on my left and the Ploggers on my right. The moon above was split in half, helping out with the darkness. We'd need that light for the letters, and we'd need the dark for the wish.

The dugout smelled like spit and sweat and grass and gum, but it had the best view of second base and the best view of home. Marcus might never have been invited into the dugout, but the way he sat up on the edge of the bench, feet on its seat, he looked more like the Skipper than ever before.

"Cool," he said.

"Gross," said Betsy, hopping over some kind of slimy goo on the floor.

I took the key off my neck and slipped it in the lock of the door Ferdie had told us about, the one next to the batting helmets. The box with the letters was on a shelf over the brooms, next to a stack of books and used-up paint cans and a pile of extra Rockskipper posters. I was lucky to have this summer's height, because I pulled it down without using Marcus as a stepping stool. That was a good thing, since he was so preoccupied.

"Can you reach those posters, Betsy?" I asked. "We need twenty-five."

While the Ploggers counted out twenty-five

posters and Marcus eyed his field of dreams, I took the letters to the steps of the dugout. The dew couldn't reach there, so it was a pretty good workspace.

"Marcus," I said, "can you find me some tape or something?"

He rummaged through a first-aid kit and tossed me a roll of medical tape. If it was sticky enough to wrap up injuries, it would be good enough for us.

"We got it, Derby." Betsy dumped twenty-five tubes on the steps of the dugout and they bounced and bumped into each other as they settled into a pile or two.

"Perfect," I said. "Will you unroll all the posters? And stack them face-down."

"Face-down? Our dads are on those things, you know," said Marcus.

"Yeah, and you know what they look like, right? We need the backs, blank."

Marcus's defense of Lump got him up off the bench, and the three of them made a stack of posters, blank-side up. I scattered the letters on the steps, searching through for the ones we needed—an *N*, a *C*, a couple *W*s. It was hard to tell if the squiggle was a comma or an apostrophe, but we'd need it, too.

We made a sort of assembly line with Ferdie's letters and the Rockskippers' posters. After I scavenged for each right letter, painted black on flimsy, clear plastic, Lollie stuck the letter on the blank side of a poster with a torn-off piece of medical tape, and Betsy laid each finished thing out along the top of the steps. They weren't as beautiful as June's sign from my first night in Ridge Creek, and they wouldn't tower over everyone like Ferdie's marquee, but they would do.

"It's perfect," I said.

"Perfect," said a Plogger.

And like he said we could have done in the first place, Marcus scrambled over the dugout and hopped into the first row. We handed him the posters letter by letter, and he stuck them under the seats in the first two rows. He only had to switch the *J* and the *U*, which made some sense because they both curved around a little.

I looked back up at the semicircle of a moon, its brightness a good sign that there wouldn't be any rain dumping down on the longest day of the year.

JUNE 21

Twenty-Eight

IN the morning, I woke up to hammering and hoots and hollers from the parking lot as the men of Ridge Creek assembled the booths and the ladies began to display their confections. But inside the Rambler, all I heard was Garland rummaging through the cabinets, rooting around for that Santa Claus mug.

"Morning, gentlemen," I said to the boys, slipping into a seat at the table. Peter crawled around on top of it, eye-to-eye with Triple, ready perhaps for the afternoon's race. I made a mental note to clean the table real good when the day was over, but first I'd keep my mouth shut and let Triple focus.

We both had a big day.

"How about some eggs, Derby?" Garland asked.

"Yes, please. And some coffee?" I turned to Triple, though I was really asking myself. "Are you ready?"

This got a crinkly, freckly morning grin out of him, and soon the three of us sat there in comfortable quiet, eating eggs and listening to the booms and bangs from outside.

"Looks like Peter's hungry." Triple grabbed one of his new drums and plopped Peter down into it, then reached for that old pistachio bag with the stadium's smorgasbord right inside. And off he went, taking all the confidence in the world with him.

Garland shouted a *Good luck!* and a *See you at the race!*, but I was too nervous for words to come out. After Triple left, Garland gave me a look that was a little bit strange and a little bit sad, and it was a hard one to read.

"I'm going to see if Marcus needs any help," I said. "Turf management, you know."

Since I wasn't really going to see Marcus, I snuck over to the Grill and twisted out a strand of lights and a garland of greenery. June needed a better wreath, and one that I could weave from spare joy might sweep away those cobwebs.

The weight of wishes and a day that would bring blisters was already bearing down, hot and humid and heavy. But the Rally didn't know about all of that, and our front yard was already almost as exciting as a nail biter of a ninth inning.

"Goose! I need the award ribbons for the pies—where are the ribbons for the pies?" Candy Plogger screeched out orders in a voice that clamored above the rest of the clatter. Goose followed her with an armful of tools and a can of paint that dripped Rock-skipper red, which made him look like a walking storage shed. Scooter followed close behind both of them, laughing and cutting up and carrying on.

That's when I understood where Betsy might have gotten her bossy from. But because sometimes the worst in people gets flipped around, I walked over to the girls' parking-spot nail salon.

"Good morning, you two," I said. "Thanks for staying here to keep an eye on June."

Lollie and Betsy were both in pink again, but not pajamas this time, and Betsy had her chopped hair floofed up and a bow stuck somewhere in the pinned-back curls. If I had been interested in having my nails painted, these two looked like experts.

"Actually, Derby," said Betsy, "I've got some business to take care of, so June is up to Lollie."

For a second, split like last night's moon, I saw the old Betsy, the one cracking bubblegum on the porch of the Sweet Street Mart. And then she ran off, like she'd forgotten all about the letters and the late night and the real Rally plans.

"Okay," I said, and I watched her go.

"It is," said Lollie. "Really."

There weren't any more seconds to split, so I thanked Lollie again and dashed down past third base, headed to June's. I took one more look at Ferdie's marquee, the one that said nothing more than **RALLY** because we'd borrowed so many letters, and all my wishes turned into hope.

I hoped Marcus was already there.

I hoped Betsy hadn't run off with my friendship.

I hoped Garland wouldn't find the Franklin bucket in my queen room.

I hoped June felt loved and needed and at home.

I still hoped the sun could stay out longer and longer and that this summer wouldn't ever end.

But when I passed the impatiens at the end of the drive and ran straight on past the weeds to the porch, Marcus wasn't there.

He'd promised. And I don't know if it was the heat or the heartache or the *Blue cow*, but I sat down on the porch, too tired to cry. I wondered how one person would pull all these weeds and pour in new dirt and clear the vines that hugged the walls.

One person can't make up a house. June couldn't keep up with this one, and maybe it was from loneliness more than needing muscles. But neither one of us could manage this job without the grounds crew.

It only takes one person disappearing for a whole family to crumble.

But then a rumble motored down the driveway. Marcus looked surer than he had the first time I'd seen him driving Franklin's cart, like now he knew he belonged there.

"I had to take the long way, remember?"

Seeing Marcus reminded me of what mattered. The crumble is quick to fix when you let other people patch it up.

"I brought you some batting gloves Lump loaned me," he continued. "I know you hate getting blisters."

And then, all of the too-tired-to-cry from earlier caught up to me and didn't stop.

"Pull it together, Lefty. It's four hours until the race. We've got to get this done." Marcus whacked me on the arm like any skipper would.

I'd already known Marcus took dirt real serious,

but then he hauled out two huge bags of soil that were each about the size of a pillowcase.

"We'll need one of those over by the mailbox and one down there by the porch," he said.

I slipped Lump's batting gloves on and dragged each bag to their new garden beds, then headed right back to the Skipper for the next call.

"These things are called sweet peas, which sounded like something June would call you, so I thought you'd both like them." Marcus handed me a box overflowing with small purple poofs. "The guy at the store even said the more you cut, the more they grow, and I thought that would be real nice for June. I used some of my grounds-crew money."

I sniffed that sweet pea, and I knew Marcus was right. And then we got to work.

Marcus said I was a natural with garden tools. I think that's probably because I'm pretty good with both a spatula and a saw, so I'm not sure why he was surprised. We yanked and dug and raked and planted, and four hands and a couple hours later, June's storm was starting to clear out.

As nice as lemonade and oatmeal raisin cookies

sounded, Marcus's company was just as good for a break, and so we settled on the front porch steps to watch the flowers and the time.

But then Betsy skipped down the driveway, waving with one arm and hauling something heavy in the other, and I remembered all that hope.

"Sorry I'm late. I had to chase down some paint." Betsy lifted up a bucket, and something sloshed over the edges.

"Paint?" I asked.

"The best pink." She nodded toward June's front door, the one whose welcome had withered. That's when I noticed that Betsy had changed into an old Rockskippers jersey of Scooter's, and she was ready to get to work. "Goose had all that red paint, and I asked Ferdie if he could spare any of that white we saw in the dugout, and he didn't even look at me funny." Betsy dug into each pocket for a paintbrush. "I bet he wondered what I needed with a bunch of billboard paint, but he gave it to me anyway and I said thank you, of course, because people are a lot nicer when you're nice to them first."

That's when I hugged her.

The Skipper took charge of finishing up the planting, either because that's who he was or because he wanted his tools back or because he didn't know what to do with all of this niceness. But still, I squeezed Betsy so tight that I got sweet-pea dirt all over her, and then we painted June's door the best pink.

Twenty-Nine

THAT might have been the best Rally ever, the one when Betsy Plogger painted a front door pink instead of painting some fingernails. The one when Marcus snuck the cart out of the stadium and drove a bunch of sweet peas around the long way. The one when Betsy insisted we do the outfielders' leap and chest bump, the one that took three people, instead of a high-five, which was just for two. The Rally I'd skipped most of — except for the turtle race.

After watching the paint dry enough so we could loop those lights and greens on the door, Betsy and I ran back to the Rally just in time for Triple's big moment. The turtles raced the length of a parking space, the one reserved for the Ridge Creek Rockskippers Fan of the Month. I think it's a parking-space-sized course mostly because you can't trust turtles to race in a circle, and besides, the Rally only lasts for one afternoon.

"On your mark!" the shortstop shouted.

"Hey," I whispered to Garland, who'd gotten there first.

"We have to chat," he said, and there was that face again.

"Get set!"

Marcus slipped up behind Triple to see how his grass cuttings had helped, and to cheer on his team. And Triple was channeling focus from somewhere any skipper would appreciate, and not even Charlie's wiggling, giggling, and gum-smacking would break that.

"I always beat you, Triple Clark, and this time I'm buying a bunny with my prize money," Charlie said, inspecting her Lollie-done manicure more than her turtle at the starting line. "I'm retiring at the end of today, though. It's kinda boring to win all the time."

Triple must have gotten his fierce determination from Garland, because he didn't budge. And when the keep-your-mouth-shut-before-getting-too-feisty gene was passed out in our family, he got all of that, too. I sure didn't. I swallowed some hot air and almost spit out a bunch of salty words to tell her what she could buy with that prize money.

And then I stopped, but only because Garland said, "Derby?"

"Okay—" I said, figuring I could explain about the stolen lights and greens.

"Aren't we lucky," he said, "getting to be front-row spectators of the greatest upset of all time?"

And we were.

It was a thrill when the shortstop yelled, "GO!" but it hit with a bit of a thunk, since turtle races aren't the speediest of events. But still, we stood there, Garland and I, cheering for Peter like he was bracing for a collision at home plate. Triple and the Skipper shouted so long and loud that between the two of them, I was sure they'd have half a voice the next day.

Twelve minutes and forty-nine seconds later, Peter tappety-clawed over the finish line, first.

Triple gripped Peter's belly and held him high up in the air, and Marcus was the first to congratulate them. And then those two boys did the rowdiest Rockskipper high-five that the James Edward Allen Gibbs Stadium had ever seen.

"So?" Triple said when he saw my shock at his newfound skill. "You said to go see Marcus in the bullpen!"

Marcus laughed and shrugged, and my heart was a jumbled-up bunch of awe at seeing the two of them, almost like brothers. Yet when I caught Garland's eye, I knew we were a strum that didn't really sound right. I followed him back to the Rambler, turning my head to watch the Skipper lead Triple and Peter on a victory lap.

I swore I heard some thunder.

Garland stepped in first and put on a kettle of water. I stood there, watching him, waiting for the storm.

"Derby," he said again, like he wanted to fill each syllable, each time, with all the disappointment that could fit. And he was patient, too, sifting through the dishes for the Santa Claus mug. He hummed something that sounded like "Take Me Out to the Ballgame," although he matched Miss Houston for mastery of the pitch. The squeal of the teakettle was a welcome note.

I couldn't find words and I'd forgotten how to wish. Garland set two mugs down on the table, stuck a teabag in each one, and filled them to the brim with hot water. Then he slipped into a seat at the kitchenette table and waited. But not for long, because Garland was the kind of dad who knew how to love, and when he put his arm up on the back of the bench, I snuck in underneath.

"Aren't we lucky, the three of us?" Garland asked. The water was too hot, so I couldn't sip the tea to stall the time and that question.

After he cleared his head and his throat, he spoke again. "But it's come to my attention that some Clark family business has been a smidge out of character." Garland's voice dropped an octave from seriousness. "Even downright sneaky. Not at all like the rambler that I know."

I let the steam smack me in the face. "Garland—" I started, not too sure what I would say next.

"Being a rambler on the road means three things." And then he paused for dramatic effect, like always. "Food, family, and fun."

That's when I knew this wasn't about taking the lights from the Grill. Garland wanted to let me steep with my thoughts and the tea. But he was as gentle as Triple was sweet, and his words made honest come tumbling out.

"I took some of the tips. I stole from us for June Mattingly," I said. "And I broke a promise to Triple and I lost Twang and I stole a strand of lights, too."

Garland lifted his mug with one hand, because the other was still on the arm that was around me. "Well, Derby," he said, as cool as the tea wasn't, "sometimes big hearts make bad decisions."

And there we were, just two ramblers with big and broken hearts. He might have been right about the lucky part, because at least with family, you can share the pieces. Our silence was interrupted only by another low rumble of thunder, one that sounded far off. I wished and hoped and wished again that it would stay there, because a storm wasn't welcome on this game day.

"I skipped most of the Rally because we fixed something special up for June at her house. But I thought she also deserved a fan or something so she wouldn't sweat her insides out. I needed money, and that's what my bad decision was all about," I explained. "But I don't even have enough. And I shouldn't have taken it."

Garland shifted, and looked up like he was asking the sky for a wish of his own.

"But you," I said. "Why do you always skip the Rally except for Triple's part? I know you love Candy Plogger's Famous Apple."

Garland set his Santa Claus mug down, and his faraway look drifted a little bit closer. "Did you hear that thunder?" he asked. "The biggest thunderstorm I ever saw in my whole life happened on the afternoon of the very first Rally for the Rockskippers. You should have seen Candy Appleton—flailing around like a hen without a head, and Goose Plogger following her around like some other chicken, pecking at her leftovers. She couldn't see him, of course, 'cause she was blinded by all the details like getting tarps over the pie tables and tying up the banners. She couldn't see what really mattered. It was three Rallies later before he got her attention and made her a Plogger."

Garland paused for a minute and sort of smiled, as if his memory had been bookmarked for this moment and the pages hadn't yellowed on the edges yet. I'd never thought of Candy Plogger being anyone but Candy Plogger, and I was only beginning to understand all that Ridge Creek kept knotted up in its shared stories.

"As entertaining as the frenzy was in the parking lot over here, I wanted to see the storm from higher ground, and the best I could think of was the stadium."

"It's magical," I whispered, mostly to myself.

"Did you know there used to be some boards loose in right field? Smack dab in the middle of the Sweet Street Mart sign. They might have nailed those up by now, but it's how we all used to sneak in and play catch under the stars when the team was on the road."

I thought of the space between FILLING and BELLIES and pictured Garland sneaking in. That secret didn't only belong to me and Marcus.

"I got as high as I could in the bleachers, even though there wasn't a dry seat in the place, and waited out the storm. That's where I met your mama. She was already up there, watching the storm roll in — beat me to the idea by who knows how many raindrops."

That ringing in your ears that happens between the burst of lightning and a crash of thunder — that was the *thing* vibrating all through my body. Garland had never told me this story before, and it settled like a bellyache.

June and Franklin had second base.

Garland and my mama had the nosebleeds.

"Before that night nobody had ever seen her, and a storm had to brew up to stick us together. The storm sure was slow to move in, but my love struck quick like the lightning."

And so we sat under that cloud for a while, Garland remembering and me wondering. That's where he stopped, so he didn't get to the part about why she wasn't a rambler anymore.

Sometimes big hearts make bad decisions.

Garland looked down at me. "Can I get you more tea? It costs seventeen dollars."

With that, the speck of jolly that had gone dark for a while was back. It was my mama who had some other storm to chase.

Thirty

BACK in my queen room, I unwrapped my mama's purple-and-silver scarf, the one that was usually stuffed under my mattress, and took a big sniff of it. It was one thing I could touch of hers that still traveled with me, but Ridge Creek's heat usually had no use for a scarf. Once, long ago, it had smelled like gardenias and marshmallows, but now it smelled more like stale metal.

The Franklin bucket with the money was still there. Garland must have found it and wondered and had that talk with me so I'd remember about the *family* part of things. He hadn't made me tell him all the details. But he did know the kind of heart I had.

And I knew his.

I could fix my bad decision, so I walked the Franklin money up to the safe and spun the dial.

The code and that day, they were the same. That's when I knew all of the 0621s from then on would be good ones. I'd remember the marquee that said nothing more than **RALLY** and the medical tape on the other letters and a front door that was the best kind of pink. A fan for June — well, I couldn't make that part happen now. And there weren't any pennies left to wish on.

"Don't want to dirty up a plate?" I asked, watching Garland fuel up for his night at the Grill with a pie that he must have braved the storm for.

And then I wished I had said something different, because maybe he had saved that pie for that particular day. But it turned out that he just had his mouth too full for banter, and his laugh sprayed crumbs across the table.

"Maybe our next truck should only serve pies — cherry, apple, boysenberry, lemon meringue, even mincemeat." He interrupted his train of thought for another bite.

I stuck my finger into the last untouched frontier of key lime, and agreed with him in one yum.

"Looks like the storm moved on," Garland said. "A good afternoon for a game."

I'd invited Garland to come, and volunteered Triple to sit with him in the nosebleeds. And when

I had put the tip money into the safe, three of the coins were pennies.

I wished Garland would go to the game.

I wished storms wouldn't make him so sad.

I wished Triple and I were all he needed.

And right then Marcus shouted from outside the Rambler. The game was on.

"Derby, are you ready? I have to check on the mower and make sure the bullpen's in order. I got a little behind this afternoon." A hint of Franklin showed up in his eagerness to tend to his turf. Franklin had picked a good skipper.

Garland must have heard a bit of Franklin too. "Wonder who he'll twirl around second base until forever comes?"

"Garland!" I squawked out a gasp of surprise and maybe embarrassment.

His eyes glimmered with that signature St. Nick twinkle. I swung open the door and acted like I was leaving in a huff, pausing just long enough to spruce myself up with a little Christmas Nutmeg.

"Hey, Lefty." The Skipper already had his rally cap on — inside out and sideways.

"Really, Marcus? Don't jinx this game, of all of

them." I kept up the pretending, even though I'm sure Marcus could feel my grin oozing out.

"Maybe that's true, but a little extra oomph couldn't hurt."

"Good thing you're into turf management. That job doesn't require much fashion sense."

"And your face paint has made you an instant expert, then?"

And that's how we went, back and forth to the stadium until he slipped between FILLING and BEL-LIES and I circled around to meet Betsy and Lollie at June's box office. The closer I got, the louder my heart pounded and the less I could see straight. All I could think about was the middle of the fifth inning.

"Ready?" Betsy's voice was serious.

She held out a sign we'd made the other night, one that had NOW written big on the back of the Rockskippers' lineup. It was rolled up like a sword she was taking into battle, but girls with pink fingernails don't have much sword-fighting experience, and a *Blue cow* didn't come soon enough to stop my laugh that slipped out.

"Yes, Betsy. We all are."

"Yeah, Betsy," Lollie echoed. I don't think Lollie

had ever talked like that to Betsy before. So I hugged Betsy Plogger for the second time that day, for the second time ever.

"Tonight will be perfect," I said, telling both them and the moving-away clouds that I was ready.

And then we settled into our spot behind the dugout, squatting and double-checking that the posters were all set, rising only for the national anthem and to heckle Mr. Bell. The air was heavy, like it was stuffed into a balloon and stretched too much.

We were all just waiting to burst.

Marcus's ripples in the outfield were a little bit ragged, since he'd spent most of the Rally grounds-keeping at June's instead of the stadium, but they were the most beautiful hurried-up ripples I'd ever seen. And there he sat in the bullpen, wild rally cap and all, talking about who knows what with June Mattingly. They were in good hands with each other.

Even Miss Houston's plunks felt expectant — each note hung on, not quite ready to fade away.

"You did it, Derby," Lollie whispered, maybe so Betsy couldn't hear, or maybe because she felt all that wonder.

"We did. We all did."

I twisted my neck to peer up in the nosebleeds above the third-base line, but Garland and Triple weren't there.

Mr. Bell bounded out of the dugout at the top of the fifth. "How about some of those sweet-potato fries if I strike out the side, Miss Clark?"

"Deal!"

Southpaws have to stick together, but also the quicker he could get us through the top of that inning, the closer we were to June. After one strikeout from Mr. Bell on the pitcher's mound, I made sure Betsy and Lollie knew what to do.

"Just like leading the wave. On your countdown, and on that NOW."

"Nobody better get up to go to the bathroom," Betsy said. "We need all those letters."

She was right. But she'd swapped her old bossy tone for one that sounded like it couldn't wait to be a part of something big.

"We've got you, Derby." Lollie unrolled her poster and locked arms with Betsy.

After the second strikeout and a leaping cheer from the crowd, I scooted over toward home plate and sat down on the steps right behind it.

The third batter took his time at the plate, which let me rest in the almost. The noise in the stadium fizzled and froze, and I wondered if that's what Peter had heard just before Triple snatched him from the creek — giant voices broken by a swift wind and a murmuring rush.

A couple of excruciating foul balls later, Mr. Bell pitched a changeup, low and away.

The batter whiffed, and it was time.

Thirty-One

IT was the middle of the fifth inning, and the players cleared the field. I pulled open the rip in the net, twisted through, and then snuck right up to home plate. I caught Ferdie's eye from the dugout, and he nodded at me, telling me in one swift motion that he'd told the real skipper and that nobody was going to run after me and haul me off the field.

Above Ferdie, it was Betsy and Lollie's turn. The two of them scrambled up and down the first two rows, pointing out the posters and bossing people around just enough to make sure everything was in order.

And then, just like every other evening in the middle of the fifth inning, Marcus's cart drove onto the field. But this time, the Skipper had a passenger.

June.

When Marcus approached second base, Miss

Houston's booth exploded with sounds of life and love, and it didn't matter if every other plunk was a wrong one. Marcus stopped the cart, offered his hand to June, and pulled her out for a dance. Where he was lanky and short, she was round and sure. He was no Franklin, but he was doing his best.

The stadium hummed and the crowd hushed and all of Ridge Creek watched Marcus and June, watched a tradition they didn't know they'd been waiting for.

The plan was to wait at home plate for Marcus to drive June around the bases to me, but I couldn't help it. I ran to third, wanting to hurry up those moments. Wanting to bring June home.

I wish I could've heard what he whispered to her at second, what made her throw back her head in laughter, and what made her clutch her cheeks and touch her heart. I bet it had something to do with how much he loved raking the dirt and how pretty her face paint was. Instead, I got to be a part of the stadium's sighs and *Oohs* and *Aahs*. Maybe even a sniffle or two leaked out, but at least I wasn't the only one.

And even though I wasn't waiting in the right

spot, Marcus drove June to me. Any good skipper knows how to change his mind in the middle of a game. The James Edward Allen Gibbs Stadium was on its feet, cheering from the bullpen to the nosebleeds. It was the kind of crescendo that echoes in your ears and rattles around in your rib cage. When June saw me waiting at home plate, when she really saw me, it felt like looking into a mirror. We had the same broken heart, sewn up and weaved back together.

"Well, Sugar Sue. Fancy meeting you here."

My hello was muted by her arms wrapping around me and the *One, two, three, NOW* of Betsy and Lollie far behind us.

"Oh my," June said, and I turned to see.

And there they were, Betsy and Lollie, who each waved a *W* up high. Plus a whole bunch of folks who had become the real-live marquee.

WE LOVE YOU' JUNE
WELCOME HOME

Turns out that the lady holding the squiggle thought it was an apostrophe instead of a comma and one of the Ls was upside down, but it didn't stop the letters from shouting loud and clear.

"I know you didn't want me on the front porch that first morning because of all those weeds and overgrown grasses and vines that wanted to strangle your house itself," I said. "Franklin wouldn't like me to see that."

"Derby." June looked over my shoulder at Ferdie's letters, rearranged just for her.

"And I know it's hot in there and that's why you made tomato-and-cucumber sandwiches without the stove and that's why the puddles of candle wax were stuck to your kitchen table, 'cause they'd melted under the blazes."

She squeezed my shoulder with her big hands and shook her head in that *Let me tell you something* way. "You think I would have wanted to cook anyway? It's been hotter than a sweater stitched with lava threads and buttons made of coal."

"I wish I could have fixed that part, but wait until you see everything else," I said. "We skipped the Rally to steal your home back for you."

Then June and I walked that well-worn path down the third baseline, where years and years of

Rockskippers had run before us. And together, we tagged home.

After that, we gave the field back to the Rockskippers, who saluted her in formation. June waved to everybody — from Betsy and Lollie behind the dugout all the way up to the nosebleeds, where Garland and Triple weren't. Even Ferdie stood on the steps of the dugout and tipped his hat.

All of Ridge Creek loved June. But I would be the one to walk her home to the sweet peas and the best pink door and the wreath of garland and lights. And maybe Betsy, too.

Thirty-Two

THE Rockskippers lost that game, but it didn't even matter. June waited in her box office while we returned Ferdie's letters to him, even though a couple of them had cracked a bit at the edges.

"That's okay," he'd said.

"What did you say once, Derby? Something about the pit stinks?" Betsy asked.

"Sinks. Sometimes the creek rises and the pit sinks." I was glad Marcus was still in the bullpen, because the last thing we needed was an armpit joke.

"Well." She grabbed my hand. "Looks like we got Mother Nature back in order. Calm as the creek, clear as mud. Something like that."

"Yeah," I said. "Something like that."

Before Betsy and I walked June home, I checked in at the Grill, just in case Garland and Triple wanted to come and see our handiwork in the yard. But a Closed sign dangled in the window, the only time I'd ever seen the Grill not serving burgers and fries after a game. I straightened up the greens just in case we opened up, and went to June's without them.

June hadn't spoken many words since the impromptu marquee had cheered her home, and that was okay, because Betsy had found a bunch of them. "Just wait until you see it, June," she said. "It really is the best pink."

Lollie ran to catch up with us once Candy Plogger said she could stay out late, and after the cart was tucked away for the night, Marcus joined us too. The five of us walked to her house, me and June in the lead, and the others a reach back. We didn't stop until we reached the sweet peas, and June cried and smiled and laughed all in the same breath.

I know she missed that *M*.

And then we walked down the driveway and up the steps to the porch, the porch that looked out over the most important turf that the Skipper had ever managed. June touched the pink and gave Betsy an extra squeeze.

That's when I saw them.

Garland and Triple pushed back and forth on the swing, so slow that it didn't even creak. On the planks below them was a fan, a big beige box one that looked like it would make the best kind of breeze.

"Hey there, Ms. Mattingly," Garland said. "Heck of a summer we're having, isn't it?"

"Sure is," June said. "Won't you all come in?"

Lollie and Betsy and Marcus filed in behind June, right past the wall of memories that captured Phoebe Susan herself. But I stayed behind, on the front porch with my family.

"How—" I started, but couldn't finish.

Triple stood up then, his small voice shattering the stillness.

"I heard you talking to Garland," he said.

Triple unfolded his fingers from around his turtle-race winnings, and reached it out to me. It wasn't twenty-five dollars anymore. It was only two.

"It wouldn't have been enough for a banjo anyway," he said. "But it was enough for Miss June."

"Aren't we lucky?" Garland said, nodding down toward Triple. "The hardware store stayed open even though it was a game day."

And then it was my turn for stillness. A flood of *Thank you* and *Peter* and *Garland must be proud* and *I am too* waited inside. It didn't take Triple as long as me to see the wonder of this place, the home that we have here in Ridge Creek.

But when I hugged him, all he said was "Eww."

Inside, I introduced Garland to Phoebe Susan, June's once-upon-a-time, who had come and gone from Ridge Creek even before his time there. And pretty soon we were all around the table together. The fan whirred a lullaby to our faint voices, and it blew June's hair out of place just enough to remind me that she wasn't stuck behind the glass in those photographs lining her wall. The lights were low and warm, and in the glow of the kitchen, we were a family of seven.

Even though her hair was the tiniest bit tousled, June's Christmas Nutmeg was radiant. She looked me in the heart, and then she told me the truth.

"You know, Sugar Sue," she said, "your home has wheels, but your heart has roots right here."

And with that, she made sense of all of Garland's *Aren't we luckys*. It was more than watching baseball and sunsets every night of every summer. It was a whole mess of Ploggers, the Skipper, and Ferdie's marquee letters traveling with me. Those things reached far beyond Ridge Creek's limits.

I had June, too.

"Hot stove or not, these tomato-and-cucumber sandwiches are out of this world," she continued. "Maybe I should get myself a food truck — what do you think, Mr. Clark?"

"Well, careful, Ms. Mattingly. We've got vegetables, too — have you tried our sweet-potato fries?"

"They're *vegetaaarian*," I said, reaching to remember a time when Betsy Plogger was a bubblegum-popping speed bump on the porch of the Sweet Street Mart. Turns out we had each been looking at a friend that day in the produce aisle.

I didn't sit in that thought for too long, 'cause Triple started up a tune — "*We got greens at the Grill: cucumbers before, and then pickles after, and we'll shake sweet potatoes with salt and pepperrrrrrr*—" and June was clapping to the rhythm even though it was awfully hard to find, and I had to do a *Blue cow*.

In the middle of the song, June picked up the centerpiece of Queen Anne's lace and placed the small vase in my hands.

"I've been picking a new bunch of this every day," June said. "Once she gets yanked out of the ground she's a rebellious kind of flower, wilting into white strands like spider webs in July's snow boots."

"Why?"

"She doesn't like to leave her roots. You, though," June said, "you're more like a dandelion, blown around by the wind and brightening up any kind of place, anywhere you land."

Maybe June was right. All of that rambling made for a string of pretty good traditions, ones that I was good at. Ones that Garland and Triple and I made together.

And after all, dandelions are as good for wishing as pennies.

LATER THAT SUMMER, WHEN DAYS WERE SHORTER AND ROOTS WERE LONGER

Thirty-Three

WE didn't see much of Ferdie for a while after the big night, but we'd still hear from his letters. Sometime in July, the marquee said **FOR YOUR DOLLARS AND TICKETS! STICK THIS IN YOUR BACK POCKET!** The first year the Rockskippers had given out wallets, Lump told us that some of them came with twenty-dollar bills stuffed inside. Marcus and I had lined up at June's box office that day, hours before batting practice.

They didn't.

But since Ferdie had faded back into the letters, Marcus and I still used that space between FILLING and BELLIES, and that was better anyway. Closer to the bullpen, part of the magic.

Triple decided that crawfish were far superior to turtles because one had scuttled by so fast that he couldn't even scoop it up before it was gone. He let Charlie keep Peter, because even though she said she was abandoning the sport, we didn't believe it. And it was a good thing he'd moved on to popcorn-bucket drums, because those things were waterproof on the inside and crawfish needed a little bit of the creek with them all the time.

A little bit of their home.

With her sassy new haircut and Heavens to Betsy, that Plogger became second-in-command to her Aunt Candy, plotting and planning the next great event at the Heritage Inn, which was somebody's retirement party. I knew she still bossed Lollie around some, but since Lollie had become the go-to nail painter for all the Ridge Creek ladies that would attend that retirement party, I didn't think she minded. Betsy had moved on to painting doors, anyway.

Betsy also became the third-best thing about the grease-splatters part of the year. Or maybe she tied with June for second. Marcus would always be first.

And he was the one who kept up the traditions of turf management all summer long. On some nights, when the electricity in the air was just right, he'd take a spin with June right past second base. He'd started wearing a Rockskippers jersey too, the one

Lump got him, the one that had *The Skipper* spelled across the back.

I watched the two of them, Marcus and June, from behind the dugout with the girls on the odd days, and from the nosebleeds with Garland and Triple on the evens. We Clarks were rambling souls, planting roots in the James Edward Allen Gibbs Stadium, digging into its dirt and traditions. We'd made a home there, even though we would hit the road again with the last snap of a Rockskipper's glove. We'd do it together.

And wasn't I lucky?

ACKNOWLEDGMENTS

The first thing that showed up in my heart was Garland's Grill. It didn't budge for a while, thanks to some busted wheels. But then there were some sparkling Christmas lights. There was a stadium, a turtle, and a Rambler. And then there was a girl.

All of these things make up a story. A lot of people make up mine.

Thank you, forever and always, to my mom and dad, Mary Ellen and Don Higgins. I'm so glad I was on the honor roll once upon a time and that the prize was tickets to see the Richmond Braves. That stuck. You did too. I love you.

This book is also for you, Sallie. You are a real true home with a real true heart, and isn't Edward lucky? You've filled his home with books and his heart with hope. I love you both.

To Julie Falatko, Elizabeth Stevens Omlor, and Jess Keating: You've each given me gifts of storytelling, story-keeping, and story-seeking, and in a way, that's like sharing souls, right? You take such good care of mine.

It is an honor to be a part of the literary legacy that is Houghton Mifflin Harcourt Books for Young Readers. Thank you to everyone who has loved Derby and welcomed her into your world. Special thanks to Sharismar Rodriguez and Brandon Dorman for picturing Derby more perfectly than my heart had done before.

To my editor, Jeannette Larson, thank you for looking at a lump of words and phrases and broken parts and spinning it into something beautiful. You understand both me and Derby in a magical sort of way, and I'm so very grateful.

And to my agent, Rubin Pfeffer: I'm so proud that this is our first book together. I can't read about Betsy Plogger popping her bubblegum without remembering how you knew what this story was about before I did. Thank you for your endless wisdom and love.

To everyone who reads this book, thank you for spending your time in Ridge Creek.

And to you, Alex. We'll always have baseball.